THE CURSED CROWN

MAY SAGE
ALEXI BLAKE

The Cursed Crown
May Sage as Alexi Blake
Twisted Mirth Publishing © 2021
Edited by Theresa Schultz
Proofread by MaKenzie Frazier
Cover Art by Gabriela Dea Julia
Design by The Book Brander Boutique

 Created with Vellum

For Theresa,
who favors highly proficient
book boyfriends.

STRIPPED TO THE BONE

Playing the prey was amusing, but if the idiots hunting her didn't show more respect for the woods, Rissa was going to cut off a few appendages before the night was through.

The dozen riders weren't the first to come for her since she'd retreated from her former home, and they wouldn't be the last. Some she'd killed, others, she'd led astray. These trespassers would meet their fate soon enough. For now, she was content to toy with them, leaving false trails, appearing in a grove, then high atop a hill.

Rissa couldn't begin to comprehend why they'd chosen to come for her after sundown. Only a handful of souls in the thirteen kingdoms could boast knowing her, but surely, they must have heard at least some of the rumors?

Once, there was a nightmare who loved a

king. Once, there was a king who fathered a nightmare. The story of Rissa's birth had traveled through the land like dust. A hundred years had passed and she still heard whispers of the monstrous royal child carried by the wind.

Behave, or the nightmare may kiss you, and lock your soul in the darkest abyss.

She could technically do that, if she were so inclined. Fortunately for all snorting urchins in Denarhelm, Rissa had never been fond of children. Or kisses.

And yet, despite all the talk of her wildness and her cruelty, the hunters came for her at night, when her power was at its strongest.

It made no sense. Still, she had little to occupy her time until the next full moon, so she indulged the fools who raced deeper and deeper into her demesne.

Clop-clop-clop.

A dozen horses galloped at full speed, their masters' swords lopping off whatever stood in their way.

Rissa neared the edge of the meadow she'd claimed as her home for three seasons. Last winter, she still woke to the sound of flutes and violins, within four walls of gilt, with curtains made of the finest silk, a bed carved in white stone, and buttered sweet bread waiting for her on a burnished platter. Now she had her meadow, her treehouse, and her freedom. She missed none of the delights of the Court of Sunlight.

Except for the sweet bread, perhaps.

It wouldn't do to let the brutes destroy her haven—the one place where she could be herself. She would have to face them here or hide.

Rissa's boredom and her curiosity called for the former option, but she hid all the same, blending with the shadow of a crooked aspen. Its fiery autumn leaves provided enough cover for her purpose.

There she waited, still and silent. She'd changed from prey to something else entirely.

Rissa was no noble knight, no sportsman following a set of rules of engagement. She wasn't even much of a fae, despite the fact that half of her blood sprang from the line of Mab herself. She was a wild thing, particularly when she felt cornered. In her youth, she'd been teased, insulted, pushed to the edge of wells, pricked with sharp twigs and spat on whenever the gentry's children believed they could get away with it. For a time, she'd taken it. Then she'd learned that nothing tasted quite as sweet as the fear of her enemies.

She was every bit the nightmare.

A soft, warm breeze carried the scent of the strangers before they came into view. They smelled just like any of her foes. Floral, distinguished scents pinching her nose. She wasn't fond of elaborate perfumes. Rissa had never had any strife with stinky little gnomes or forest imps. It was the gentry, the high fae, she loathed.

Though she didn't call to the power running in her blood, she could feel branches crawling along her bare skin, curving around her wrists like whips, covering her heart and throat with a thick layer of bark and moss. Under her plain green velveteen dress, an armor of wood protected her. She felt a spider move along her throat and settle on her feathered shoulder. Gently, Rissa rested her clawed hand next to it. The crawler took the invitation, rushing to her palm. She set it on the tree. She wasn't willing to involve the creatures of the woods in gentry quarrels. Their kind was too callous to those they deemed lesser than themselves.

Rissa scrutinized her enemies. Covered in black floating cloaks over bare skin and metal plates, they were dressed for battle. Two held themselves like true warriors, and six seemed to be indistinguishable lower knights. She ignored them all, dangerous as the first pair might have been.

Only one man mattered: the one riding front and center. Rissa couldn't take her eyes away.

He was a threat, the likes of which she'd never encountered in these woods.

Rydekar Bane.

She'd been a girl only fifteen years of age the

last time she'd seen him. In a century, she'd grown into a confident, powerful woman who didn't bow to anyone.

Yet her impulse was to bow to him, or dart out and run again, as far, as fast as she could.

It might have been wise. Survival dictated that she should defer to the most powerful man in the entire fae world.

She remained in the shadows, silent and still, taking in everything about him.

He'd grown too. In power and, if it was even possible, in beauty. The high fae were all beautiful, with their refined, elegant features—long limbs, flawless skin, perfect cherry mouths. He was worse than the rest—the one black rose in a sea of reds and whites.

Rydekar was bulkier than any fae had the right to be—courtesy of the human blood in his veins, presumably. His shoulders were twice as large as hers, yet he bore his massive frame with the grace of a tiger lying in wait, ready to strike an unknowing quarry.

Even as a child she'd been quite taken with his stunning amethyst eyes, so intense they seemed to peel her skin away, to get at the very core of her being. He unmade her, unwrapping all her secrets.

Rydekar wore no steel, just layers of dark clothes cut from fabric that looked both easy to move in and soft as silk. She would have given much for a yard or two of it. Sensible as it was, the clothing didn't quite seem appropriate for him. He should have been in armor or in intricate clothes stitched with gold. Something felt wrong. What was he doing here at all?

Rissa *should* flee. She would. Any moment. One step, then the next. She knew the woods better than he did. She could hide or outrun him.

She'd been mistaken to assume her pursuers were gentry from her father's kingdom, or anywhere else in the realm of Denarhelm. These hunters weren't relatives eager to get her out of the way so that they might rise higher in the line of succession, if her father never returned.

If they were led by *him*, they came from the south. From the *unseelie* world. They were dark fae, known to live in chaos, kneeling to nothing but power. *His* power. For Rydekar now bore a sharp crown of black crystal blades.

He wore it like he'd been born to it, which he had. Like Rissa, Rydekar was one of the few heirs of the high queen Mab. Unlike her, he looked the part.

His gleaming hair fell in waves, coating his tanned skin in a golden halo. His eyes shone as they scanned the darkness, seeing through flesh. In the distance, enveloped in the shadow of the woods, she should have felt safe. Invisible.

She didn't.

The unseelie king in the south had come for

her, and she'd been too foolish to flee when she had the chance.

The bright amethysts were set on her.

He stilled for a moment, and turned to observe the rest of the meadow.

She could have breathed out in relief, if she'd dared brave a noise.

"Are we to play a game?" His voice was soft, like a caress, if caresses could be cold and menacing. "You hide, and I seek. I expect a prize when I catch you."

When, not if. He didn't doubt that he'd best her. Rissa wondered if that man had ever lost against anyone.

He dismounted a great warhorse, its hide a black so smooth and incandescent she wanted to run her hand over its mane. To her surprise, Rydekar then removed his crown, then tossed it casually to one of the bare-chested warriors. The poor soul practically fell off his horse to catch it midair.

"What will it be, cousin?"

It was all she could do not to snort. They were hardly cousins. Rissa's father was the son of Mab and of the shy Alder King, who'd left the continent thousands of years ago.

Rydekar came from another line, issued of Mab's dalliances with Ovleron, long after her first mate was gone. Rissa could remember a great tapestry adorned with the family tree following that line. It covered a dozen generations, over the course of a thousand years, ending with Nyx Lilwreath, the first unseelie high queen. The Court of Sunlight had little interest in recording the rest of the family, once they'd stayed beyond the southern borders.

Rydekar was one of Nyx's descendants, born another thousand years after her. He had more blood in common with humans and pucks than he did with her.

She remained silent and still as another breeze brushed her face. The wind carried an autumn leaf through the meadow. She could have groaned.

Rydekar didn't turn back to her, though the air no doubt carried her scent.

Rissa grinned. She often expected others to share the most natural of her abilities, but unlike her, they weren't beasts. She would have immediately found him, susceptible as she was to smells.

One of the warriors inched forward, but the high king lifted a long, imperious hand, wordlessly commanding him. Though he looked quite put out, the man remained in his position, his horse's hooves tapping the ground impatiently.

Its rider was no less impatient. Rissa guessed he wasn't used to being left behind. The warrior was dark of hair and as tanned as his king. They must spend a fair amount of time in the sun. And like Rydekar, he was of a consequential build.

His impressive amount of defined muscles was covered in intricate markings that would have impressed Rissa, if she were one to be intimidated by raw strength.

She'd seen great men piss themselves in terror, though none had been quite as colossal as that giant.

The second warrior, still and silent at his side, had skin so white it looked bluish in the light of the moon, and while he bore markings too, they were of a different make than those she was familiar with. His short coral hair and moss-green eyes made for a striking picture. Almost as tall as his king, he was considerably leaner, and carried a bow across a shoulder, as well as a sword. This man was the picture of a fairy prince. Polished, thin-limbed, high-cheeked, and calculating. Instincts told her that she didn't want to ever be on the other side of one of his arrows. The giant, she could handle. The princeling felt too cold.

The other knights were cut from the same cloth, their heavy helms hiding their features. She didn't doubt they were proficient enough, as they walked with their king, but they weren't anything she hadn't faced before.

Overall, she was outnumbered, and to her irritation, outmatched too. Rissa wet her dry lips, considering.

"I can't quite remember how the game is

played. I'm supposed to count, aren't I? When I get to ten, I will find you."

A promise sharper than the edge of her knife.

Rissa swallowed a sigh and slid out of the shadows.

She fixed her attention on Rydekar, projecting a confidence she had no reason to feel, and he stared back at her, violet eyes taking in every inch of her. The plainest of her dresses, one that had seen better days—it was tattered at the hem and dusty in places. Rissa grimaced as she looked down. She would have preferred to appear in a better light, but she hadn't expected visitors when she'd awoken that afternoon. His gaze slid to the bark and feathers, the thorns, and her locks of hair, loosely tied at her waist so that it didn't get in her way.

She knew he must find her wanting. She needed a brush, a bath, a petticoat void of spider-webs. She'd long forgotten to care, and she refused to start now. Never mind the blush heating her skin.

Rydekar saw it all. His mouth stretched into a smile that didn't thaw the chill in his eyes.

"Serissa." Her name sounded peculiar in his mouth. Unfamiliar. More sensual than it had ever been. "All grown up, I see."

Oh, screw him.

TWO SIDES

Serissa Braer—heir of Mab, rightful queen of all seelie folk—stood before him for the first time in nigh on a century, at long last.

She was a mess. A mess, a waste of time, and a waste of resources.

Rydekar had been taught to hide under a mask of cultivated indifference before he took reading lessons. Detachment was his nature. He'd never been so close to losing it. He wanted to scream at her. Shake her until she gained some sense.

Her kingdom, her birthright, was being attacked, falling to pieces, and she was picking flowers in the woods.

He *hated* her. He didn't know her at all, but he hated everything she represented.

That didn't change the fact that he needed her.

"I see you're tired of sending underlings for me to play with," Serissa said lightly.

Rydekar managed a humorless chuckle. He had dispatched several trackers on her trail. Few had returned, and none had been sound of mind. "They tell me you're a tricky beast to hunt. I thought I'd give it a try. I rather like a chase."

And he had found the ride quite refreshing, given the mess he'd left behind. He would have enjoyed it far more if he could have impaled her at the end of a spear instead of playing nice with her.

"What do you want, Bane?"

Bane. She wasn't addressing him as King, Highness, or anything honorific. Rydekar was lord in the south, in unseelie territory. The Darker Woods were on seelie land, and answered to no one. His dominion ended at the border of her woods, as she was quick to remind him.

The brat.

Still, he was glad that she cut the pleasantries short. "What does any king want?"

"A beating heart for dinner? Entertainment? No, I know." Her gaze took him in from the tips of his bloodred boots to his eyes in one sweeping glance. Then she grimaced. "Better clothes. Well, I don't share my tailor. Find your own."

He was in no mood to be teased. "Power, Serissa. I want the power to protect my realm." As she should.

"It's *Rissa*." Her eyes narrowed in annoyance. "And you've come *here* to seek it?" She gestured around her, to the peaceful meadow shrouded in mist.

Didn't she see it? Didn't she realize who she was, what she was? All he saw was power when he took her in. Squandered power, thrown out like ashes in the wind.

"Rissa. I like it." He did. Serissa was the formal name, fit for a queen. Rissa felt smaller, weaker, younger. It was perfect for her. "Come closer, then, Rissa dear," he beckoned, endeavoring to be charming.

He didn't truly aim to seduce her, but if she was weak enough to fall at his feet, all the better.

Perhaps she was stupid and malleable. That would be convenient.

She didn't budge.

"I'd rather not shout royal business for all to hear." Rydekar could have joined her, but he'd much rather set a precedent and have her come to him.

"I'm quite content right here, Bane."

She wasn't going to be easy. His eyes narrowed.

"Besides," she added offhandedly, "I don't see why I should be concerned with royal business."

Rydekar breathed in and out, letting his energy flow through his mind.

No, his soothing technique wasn't working at

all with her. She was actively trying to annoy him, and it was working. "I would prefer not to be forced to make you obey me."

"Make me?" She was half amused, half astounded.

No one had ever made that brat do anything, by the looks of it. She'd been spoiled rotten, allowed to let her fancy take precedence over the state of her realm.

"Make you," he repeated, ever so softly. "I would prefer for us to have a partnership, if we can. But I'll get what I'm here for either way."

"Will you, now?" She was practically purring, enjoying the challenge.

Rydekar's patience, generally thin, had come to an end. He extended his hand, palm up, and focused on her eyes. They'd seemed brown at first glance, but now the light had changed, and he could catch some blue, some green in their ever-changing depths. Hazel.

He liked her eyes, and their endless, dark lashes. He liked the shape of her mouth, and the curve of her long neck. The teal, gray, and midnight-black feathers coating her shoulders, he simply loved. She wore them as a bride's veil, with a natural grace.

Most of the fae of his court were pleasant enough to look at. Tall and athletic, glowing with health, powdered, manicured, perfumed. Beauty was the standard, and few ever stood out.

Rissa was a raw, primal vision in the night. A striking mess, unapologetically unique. He hated her for her allure, too. Better she be homely, or at least, boring. She could have chosen to make half the world kneel at her feet, and she hadn't. She had no right to look the queen when she refused to act like it.

He did just what he'd threatened, forcing her to come to him, commanding each of her steps. For one blissful moment, he allowed himself to treat her like any enemy.

He enjoyed the fear in her wide eyes as she realized she couldn't control her body. She couldn't do anything against the compulsion, taking one step after another, until she stood right before him, as he intended.

Rydekar congratulated himself on being particularly kind. He could have made her crawl. He *wanted* to make her crawl to his feet.

The vision of the proud, unbearably bewitching royal on the ground before him was heady, haunting. He could imagine running his thumb over her lip. Making her suck on it.

Damn her for this.

"What do you want?" She was gritting her teeth, each word a dark curse.

Still tormented by thoughts of her less defiant, less unmanageable, obeying him willingly, Rydekar was done smiling.

He dropped the pretense, his eyes flashing

with a raw need, giving her a glimpse of the monster beneath his suave demeanor. "You," he told her honestly. Too honestly. "Where you belong."

In that instant, he wondered if she understood him perfectly. Anger fired in those annoyingly enticing eyes, and she managed to step back.

On your knees.

Rydekar had to get back into focus. He wasn't here to find a sheath for his cock, no matter how perversely tempting *Rissa* Braer was. "On the throne of Denarhelm."

He could tell he'd surprised and confused her.

What did you expect of me, dearest?

"There's no throne of Denarhelm," she replied, attempting for neutrality, but he could tell she was piqued now.

Rissa was showing her teeth. Her canines were starting to point. The useless princess had fangs, at least.

Somehow, that ended up infuriating him even more. She had guts. She *could* take the crown. She could demand it and have the thirteen lords swear to her. She was truly indifferent and unwilling to save her people—to save the fae!

He snapped. "There could be, if you weren't a spineless, worthless waste of space."

Rydekar had never lost his grip on his temper in public—not once in his three hundred years. Nothing had ever incurred his wrath as much as this woman, and her lack of responsibility.

To his surprise, she laughed. "I've heard worse." She didn't so much as take umbrage at the insult, letting it roll off her feathers.

She was used to this, he realized.

Rydekar wondered who'd dared denigrate her before. More importantly, he wondered why he wanted to crush their skulls in his grip. Given the fact that he'd been so quick to spew curses at her, he could hardly blame those who'd come before him.

Reason be damned. He'd kill anyone who dared treat her as anything less than what she was—Mab's granddaughter.

If she didn't have the respect of the folk, he had no use for her.

"Get out of my woods, Rydekar. You're on seelie land, and you're not welcome. I'll gladly drag you myself." She sounded tired now. Fed up with him for taking up her time.

As though she had aught else to do here. He grinned, imagining what she might have planned for the rest of the night. Sniffing mushrooms? "Unlikely, but I'd enjoy your attempt."

Her hazel eyes burned bright. He could clearly sense it—she imagined freezing him in place and extracting every dram of pain and agony from his mind. Her fantasy would remain in her imagination. Unlike hers, his mind was warded against intrusions.

Rissa was unprepared, untrained, undisciplined. Everything he despised.

But she also was the one person who could rise to take the crown of the seelie world. Her father had disappeared. There was no one else alive in the line of Mab. No one with seelie blood. All fae needed her to find some form of courage and nobility.

He tried using reason. "You must know Antheos's army is already on seelie territory. Every day, they take another town, another village at your western border, encountering no true resistance. They're marching on the kingdom of Denarhelm first because you're vulnerable. It's easy pickings. I could claim it tomorrow if I so wish."

"There is no *kingdom* of Denarhelm," she repeated, stubborn to the last. "The thirteen courts have ruled independently since the days of Queen Una."

Accurate enough. The seelie kingdom had long been divided into minor courts. The last high queen ruling over them all left the throne vacant. Perhaps for valid reasons at the time, but almost two thousand years later, the world had changed. A wind of blood and iron had blown through the continent for some time, and now war was upon the fae lands.

Rydekar had long looked north, watchful, perhaps even hopeful. Seelie were known to be creatures of wisdom and honor. He'd believed they'd do the right thing: ally to strengthen themselves.

Instead, he'd heard that King Titus, the one child of Mab still alive, had left his Court of Sunlight. Mere months later, his only child, Serissa, disappeared too.

Rydekar's best trackers hunted both. His knights only found the daughter.

He took their actions as a personal betrayal. So much selfishness, narrow-mindedness, and careless disregard for their duties was a disgrace.

Rydekar tried to remain as calm as he could manage to be. He needed this conversation to go well. He needed her to follow him. He needed her to step into the role the Fates had paved for her. "A divided kingdom without a leader is weak. If you do not rise now, you will fall. You will fail." He took one step forward to close the distance between them again, and leaned in. "You will all die without my kindness, little girl."

Rydekar generally concealed the extent of the power he held in his grasp. Not only could he control the minds of others, he was also strong enough to affect the elements around him. Right now, he was letting her feel every single bit of his strength.

He expected her to falter, shiver, drop her gaze to the ground, like the flock of gentry buzzing around him. If she recognized his strength, she was more likely to accept his protection.

She surprised him again. "Kindness?" Rissa snorted. "Why did no one think to tell me you had any?"

She wasn't weak at all.

Just selfish.

"I have none. You will beg nonetheless."

I just may, in his dreams. And in my nightmares.

Rydekar blinked, and took a step back.

Her thoughts.

He could feel her thoughts, as clearly as if they'd come out of her mouth, though her lips had remained stubbornly closed.

He looked down and realized he'd taken her hand, closing his fingers around the small wrist.

He didn't like it, but a mental link wasn't unheard of. They were both descendants of Mab, and though she didn't seem to care one way or the other, they were the seelie and unseelie monarchs by bloodright. Both sides of the same coin.

"I'm giving you a chance to join me on your terms. My high court has moved to the Old Keep, in the Murkwoods. We've sent word for what's left of your courts to make for the borders with their forces. Your numbers aren't enough to push against all of Antheos." To his annoyance, he had to admit, "Nor are mine. When they come for Tenebris after destroying your land, I may be victorious, but there will be too many losses among my people. We have to ally, and prepare to beat our common enemy back to their borders."

Old Keep was the best place for this. The ancient castle had been built in another era, when all fae had stood together under Mab's rule, before the courts parted ways. It was deep inside the Murkwoods, right at the edge of the seelie and unseelie lands.

Rydekar had moved there the moment his spies had alerted him that Antheos was gathering their armies.

Antheos, the land to the west.

Antheos had attacked the fae world twice already. They'd failed in the time of Rydekar's ancestors, and he was not going to let them take their border now.

Even if he had to drag this princess to a throne, tie her up, and shove a crown on her head.

That notion didn't lack merit.

"If I have to treat you like a puppet, you won't like the position I put you in."

She lifted her chin. "And what, pray, would I do, in Old Keep?"

Was she mentally challenged? That seemed obvious. "Rule."

COMPROMISES

Rissa had been told time and time again that her temper would get her into trouble someday. She was fairly certain that Miss Prott—her yellow, rumple-skinned old imp of a governess—must have been talking about this day, in an uncharacteristic show of clairvoyance.

Her temper was going to make her throttle the high king of Tenebris and start a bloody war if he didn't get out of her face, out of her meadow, out of her woods, and out of her life.

Ruling? Absurd.

She snatched her hand out of his grasp. "I think I'll pass."

Her instincts urged her to face her enemy, keep her eyes trained on his every movement, but she turned away. She was fairly certain he would take it as a slight, a lack of respect, and that was exactly the feeling she wished to convey.

How *dare* he come here and attempt to dictate her life?

"You'll...pass."

She walked with her head held high, refusing to spare him a glance, though she could feel his anger coating her like a living thing. A bright flame, washing over her in waves.

"Thousands of fae dying, children, elderly, innocent, and weak, and you'll *pass*?"

Rissa would have preferred if he'd shouted. The deliberate, slow whispers were worse.

Now, she spun around. "You have no clue what you're asking of me. You know nothing about me. And trust me when I say, you know nothing about Denarhelm."

If he believed the thirteen lords would accept *her* as their high queen, he was deluded. The very fact that he considered it a possibility was bizarre.

Bizarre and flattering. No one had ever believed her capable of ruling anything—not even her own life. Secretly grateful for the vote of confidence, Rissa couldn't help a tiny little pang of appreciation for the pushy, rude, self-important jackass of a king.

And that had nothing to do with the fact that he was so beautiful looking at him made her dizzy.

"You live like a hag in the woods rather than facing your responsibilities. I know you're a coward."

I have no responsibilities, save those you'd force on my shoulders. Just because you believe they belong to me doesn't make it so.

That was what she wanted to say, and she parted her lips to deliver it sharply. No word crossed her lips, though. For better or worse, she was fae, and since the dawn of time, the folk had been cursed with the inability to lie.

Rissa paused, shocked to find that she couldn't speak up. If she'd *truly* believed her words, true or false, they would have spilled out of her mouth. Why would any part of her think the fate of Denarhelm was her business?

The answer came to her too readily. She was Mab's heir. Mab's *granddaughter*. She was High Queen Una's niece. *If* there had been a crown of Denarhelm, in her father's absence, it would have belonged to her.

She could feel her shoulders sag as fight left her bones, her fury receding.

Rydekar might have been unbearably cruel in coming to her, but he didn't know that. The only thing he knew was that she was next in line to bear the crown. To be rid of him, she had to explain herself.

The words were hard to say. Even after all this time, they were hard to swallow, to accept.

She forced them out. "I live here because I'm not wanted in the Court of Sunlight. And I would certainly not be wanted anywhere near a high throne, if we had one."

"Not wanted?" Rydekar pushed.

Of course he wouldn't leave it alone. This king was a dog with a bone. He had probably never left anything alone in his entire life.

"In case it escaped your notice, I'm not exactly what one would consider the typical fair fairy princess." Her tone was clipped.

Rydekar truly seemed confused, as though he hadn't seen the feathers and bark, the fangs and claws. The wildness. "You must be joking."

He didn't believe her, that much was clear.

Rissa laughed. This man, this king, was pure perfection from head to toe. The seelie courts would have worshipped the ground he walked on, even if he had no crown to lord over them. And yet he couldn't see why they'd reject her.

A few moments ago, she would have been happy to set him on fire. Now she could have kissed him.

"The seelie court doesn't do well with anything unconventional," she proffered in explanation.

Though her attention remained fixed on the king, she didn't fail to notice the two warriors, still mounted on their horses, exchanging a glance. They got it.

Her jaw set when she recognized their expressions. She didn't need any pity.

His mouth thinned. "They'll bow to you. They don't have a choice. The crown belongs to you."

In what universe did he live? "No, they won't. They're great lords, with greater armies, and no one has made them do anything for thousands of years. They like it that way."

Rydekar glanced back to his men. The pale warrior trotted to join him, needing no further prompting. "From what I know of seelie law, the lords can vote an unsuitable monarch off the throne, if they're unanimous. The reason doesn't matter. So long as they agree, they could cast her out."

Rissa hadn't known that.

She couldn't say she liked realizing how little she knew about her own lands, to be entirely honest. The fact that she had no interest in claiming a crown didn't mean that she shouldn't be aware of how the seelie land functioned.

And she should also have known that they were under attack. She couldn't do much about it, but hearing the news from a stranger was a blow. No one had thought it necessary to keep her informed. Not even the few she counted as friends.

"How do you know that?" Rissa questioned.

He wasn't seelie, and they were known to guard their secrets jealously.

The stranger looked to the king first. Rydekar gave a subtle nod. Now that he was permitted to speak, he explained, "I'm of the Sea Land." He gallantly inclined his head. "We're taught the laws of every fae court as children."

A custom the rest of the folk should adhere to. "I see. Well, then that's sorted." She could return to her treehouse, and her peace. "Take care on your way back."

"You can't mean that." The second warrior approached, frowning. "They need unanimity. Surely you have allies who—"

"I don't." Not among the high lords. Not among the gentry. Not among anyone who mattered.

Which was a moot point, because Rissa had no desire or intention of claiming any crown.

"The one thing they'll all agree on is that I'm an unsuitable ruler. I doubt they'd accept anyone at all, save Tharsen himself." Rissa had thrown the name out thoughtlessly, but now she paused. "Wait. You need someone to unite the seelie kingdom..."

Like any child of the folk, she'd been nursed to rhymes of the cursed prince, alone in the depths of the Wilderness, awaiting his deliverance.

Rissa looked straight at Rydekar, who stared,

silent and foreboding. "That's who you need. Prince Tharsen."

Children's tales weren't always fabricated.

Prince Tharsen was High Queen Una's own son, raised to take over as high king of Denarhelm. The year he was supposed to take the crown from his aging mother, a terrible sickness ravaged the land, killing thousands of folk. The prince used all of his magic to fight it, till he was so depleted he would have died. His mother managed to save his life, but he never woke.

Many attempts were made on his life, so the queen had his body removed to the heart of the Wilderness, where no ambitious heir could reach him, until he could acquire enough energy to be reawakened.

She died soon after, leaving the throne vacant —and vacant it had remained since.

Prince Tharsen had slept for almost two thousand years.

"Is it?" Rydekar asked.

She couldn't even begin to read his features when he was this quiet, this calculated, but for some reason, Rissa had a feeling that he was angry again.

No, not angry this time. His anger had felt like a hot, smoldering embrace, ready to consume her.

This was cold.

This was...worse.

"The lords would bow to Tharsen," Rissa insisted. "They'd rally to him. If anyone can defend our land, it's a prince raised to lead our armies."

"Hm." Rydekar was a tomb.

Until now, his presence had been a force taking over the whole meadow. He was gone, his eyes vacant. Indifferent.

"I could go." Animated, Rissa nodded. She was growing more and more convinced by the minute, and she desperately wanted Rydekar to agree with her, though she'd be hard-pressed to explain why. "I could wake him. It'd be best for everyone."

The king's darker warrior remained out of the meadow, but his voice traveled the distance with ease. He must have been taught the art of oration, like most noble children. "Princess, Tharsen's as north as it goes, behind a hundred tribes of wild folk, the Hunt, and dragons, if rumors are right." He chuckled, shaking his head. "You wouldn't manage it. Not with an army. There's a reason no one has attempted to seek him out yet."

Rissa glared at him. "No one has attempted to seek him out because the lords didn't want or need a king until now." She turned to Rydekar. "If the situation is as desperate as you say it is, Tharsen is your best hope. And I won't need an army. I'll go alone." She lifted her chin. "I'm a nightmare."

Nightmares, or *mara*, were an old kind of folk —one of the first to ever roam the lands. There were few of them left, and all of them lived in the Wilderness.

Except her.

Rydekar snorted. "A half-nightmare, at best." He paused. "But I suppose the wild folk may not attack you on sight. If you wish to go north, I cannot stop you."

Part of her wanted to point out he couldn't stop her from doing anything at all. He wasn't her king, or anything else to her. But the memory of the way he'd made her come to him, his violet eyes brightening as the compulsion moved her limbs, made her shut her mouth.

Choose your battles wisely, Rissa. Now wasn't the time to push him again. "I'm not asking for your blessing."

"Excellent. You do not have it."

Infuriating man.

"We'll play this game, as you insist. Go north. Find your lord and savior." There was something dark in his voice. "Let him steal the crown from you, if you so wish. But first, you'll travel with me to the Old Keep. Already, seelie folk are coming to us for shelter or guidance. The lords have sent ambassadors. You *will* stand beside me, and present a united front to your people and mine, so that the world sees you're fighting this war with us. It'll go a long way to smooth the relationship between our two kingdoms. Do this, and I'll provide whatever support necessary for your journey."

She considered each word.

More orders. Rissa didn't like his tone, but she supposed the arrogant bastard couldn't help it. He was used to people jumping at the snap of his fingers.

"Fine," she finally said. So long as there was no more talk of slapping a crown on her head, she was winning. "But you're going to have to stop ordering me around if you want people to believe I have any sort of authority."

Rydekar snorted. "I'll give that all due consideration."

That was a no, then.

"You're a bastard, Rydekar Bane."

He snorted. "With any luck, you're right."

DANCE OF SNAKES

"Let us make haste. We've wasted enough time here." Rydekar turned his back to her, silently conveying just how little he thought of her, like she had moments ago.

They'd agreed to an alliance of sorts, but they were far from friendly, and he had no reason to trust her. From her, the slight had been minor, but men like him didn't present their back to a potential enemy, unless they considered them entirely useless.

The *audacity*. He made her itch to reach for the dagger strapped to her ankle and throw it right between his shoulder blades. If Rissa stayed her hand, it had more to do with the pale warrior's cold eyes set on her than with her inclination.

The king reached his dark horse, mounted it

deftly, and stared pointedly at her. *"Any time now would be good."*

Ignoring the grating impatience radiating off Rydekar, Rissa crossed the clearing, heading for her tree.

His highhandedness made it absolutely essential for her to take twice as much time as she otherwise would have.

"Tough. You will wait for me." He hadn't crossed onto seelie land and hunted her down in person to leave her behind. "I have personal effects to retrieve."

And she needed to get changed, badly. She was familiar enough with the ways of the courts to know her attire would be inappropriate, even for a lowly chambermaid.

He snorted, no doubt questioning what sorts of things kept in a treehouse could be worth the bother.

Many might have surprised him. Rissa's space was littered with priceless—and worthless —jewels, spelled stones, dresses of the finest silk, and goblets of carved gold.

While she enjoyed the simplicity of life in the woods, she still liked pretty things to look at. She wouldn't have wanted to leave her favorite baubles behind, in the Court of Sunlight, when she had no intention of returning to her former home anytime soon.

Rissa deftly climbed her beech tree, her feet and hands grabbing onto the familiar nooks and crannies of its branches and trunk, till she reached the cluster of boughs where she'd built her house.

It was rather simple. A floor made of smooth planks, a curtain of knotted vines, and a roof of polished ash. More spacious than one would have thought, the circular room was spelled to stay warm and dry in the winter, and to keep strangers out when she wasn't here. Not the best at domestic enchantments, Rissa had spent weeks working out the kinks of that trick. She'd built the small, carved bed, and painstakingly filled the mattress with wolf fur, earning a bite or two in the process.

An old gray and silver tapestry served as a rug, while another hung on the wall closest to her bed, to keep the sunlight out. She often slept during the day.

Trinkets covered every surface, her favorite ones displayed on makeshift tables and cabinets. She'd built almost everything here, over the course of the last century. Even back when she officially lived at court, she used to retreat to the woods and come here whenever she could.

The treehouse was far from a palace, but it was all hers. Her sanctuary. It smelled of apple, pine, lily of the valley, and home.

Rissa shed the dusty greenish dress she wore most days, and moved to the basin filled with fresh rainwater to freshen up. She stilled and put the soft cleaning cloth back on the lip of the basin. "I wouldn't have pegged you as a voyeur."

After today, Rissa suspected she would be able to sense Rydekar's distinctive presence anywhere. Not only because of his unique scent —white-hot crackling embers, along with a purely masculine tone of leather, mud, and cold spices. No, she recognized him because, while there was one person, he felt like an entire army stood in his shadow. Power. It radiated off him. Rydekar wore it as a second skin.

"What would you have pegged me as?" His voice felt like a caress along her bare skin. She hated herself for reacting to it.

"I'm getting changed." Point for stating the obvious... "If I wanted you here, I would have invited you."

"Let's not pretend you have any clue what you want, Rissa dear."

Smug bastard.

She fixed her narrowed eyes on him. To her annoyance, he'd invaded her space like he belonged there, sitting on her narrow, unmade bed. He looked entirely out of place, his frame so large it made it look like a child's cot.

Suddenly aware of her near nakedness, and

of his bright violet eyes set on her, she had to resist the impulse to hide under her washcloth.

Ridiculous. She'd ended up dancing naked at several celebrations and had been indifferent to the eyes of the court. Everyone was uninhibited and in various states of undress by midnight on solstices.

Tonight wasn't a solstice, and she wasn't nearly drunk enough to withstand the heat and scrutiny of his attention.

Free of her dress, she stood in a tunic so thin it did nothing to conceal her shape. Its back dipped low enough to hint at the curve of her ass. Underneath, weapons adorned her—a dagger at the right ankle, a knife around the left thigh, and an assortment of potions and explosives in flasks and pouches belted at her hips. She itched to throw all of them at his placid, infuriating face.

Rydekar looked at her without even attempting to disguise his inspection, as though he had every right to feast his eyes on her curves, yet he did so with a nonchalance and indifference that got under her skin more than anything he'd said and done until now.

Rissa felt her skin prickle. Glancing down, she noticed vines curling around her wrists, ready to defend her. Saving the insults she wanted to throw at Rydekar for later, she focused on her arms, sending soothing vibes until the vines stopped gathering at her palm, and faded back under her skin.

"Does this happen often?" Rydekar asked.

She shrugged, not gracing him with an answer.

"You wear nature itself in your veins. Do you ever wonder what power you could wield, if you only wanted to?" His tone was cutting.

Rydekar seemed angry, which amused her greatly. Rissa found that she liked to annoy him nearly as much as she would have liked to throw one of her knives at his pretty face.

Most people feared, or were disgusted by the wilderness inside her, never far from the surface, but unless she was mistaken, she read something very different from him.

Envy.

Naturally, Rissa latched on to it. "Does it frustrate you? That I have a power you don't possess."

She knew the answer, but asking him made her triumph complete.

His curt chuckle held no humor. "There's nothing about you that doesn't frustrate me." He sighed, stuffing his hands in his pockets in a gesture uncharacteristically casual. Then, he reclined on her bed, throwing his head back. "Dress, if you must. I want us to reach the keep before the court sleeps. The sooner you're intro-duced, the sooner you can leave."

Rissa didn't quite know what to make of him like this. His eyes weren't attacking her, he wasn't biting her head off or insulting her for the moment. He just looked tired. Rydekar seemed younger, smaller. Almost vulnerable.

Well, she could hardly argue against him, when she very much wanted to spend as little time as possible among the gentry. They should leave soon. Yet, she found that she wanted to contradict him on principle. He'd given her yet *another* order, and she was determined to never obey this arrogant fae king. "Didn't your father tell you not to rush a lady?"

He never moved, never so much as looked at her. "I swear I will throw you over my shoulder, drag you down and strap you to the back of my horse if you persist in testing me." His voice remained calm and collected. She wondered how much practice he must have had at hiding his rage.

Because he was furious. She could sense it, taste it.

And she relished it.

She shrugged. "You can try."

She shouldn't have pushed—not after the way he'd controlled her earlier. She knew what sort of predator she was dealing with. The problem was that he truly saw her as nothing more than an annoyance, a small, weak girl he could manipulate. That had to end. Right now.

Her every instinct told her to show him just what a nightmare was.

She could barely see him move, but the energy in her room crackled, and the next instant, he was flush against her, his warm, hard skin on hers, his hands around her waist. He lifted her up.

She smirked. "I've got you."

Her hands moved to either side of his face and she leaned in, as if to kiss him. Rydekar's eyes widened.

Just as her lips closed in on his, she opened her mouth and sucked in his dreams.

She could taste them. The memories of joy, of peace and happiness. The laughter of a child and the songs of a mother. A first kiss, promises whispered in the woods. Everything that made him hope and love the world—love himself.

Most people were focused on their own happiness, their own needs. Rydekar's dreams were for the betterment of his people. He dreamed of a festival where all laughed and danced without fear for tomorrow. He dreamed of his throne being secure. The lords bowing to him, and a queen at his side.

She was nondescript. She could have been anyone, anything. What mattered was that they bowed.

Rissa's curiosity made her focus on the

queen. She could distinguish the hint of her long, dark wavy hair.

"Enough!" The scream pulled her out of the dream.

Back in her treehouse, she faced Rydekar, who didn't look nearly as collected as he had before.

His eyes, the only expressive things about him, had dimmed dangerously. Rissa couldn't decide whether they were too cold or too warm. Perhaps a strange, explosive mixture of both.

Letting go of her, Rydekar took a step back, panting.

Finally. Finally, he was treating her like his equal. Something to be feared. Something to be *respected*.

Rissa was seldom respected. Acknowledged, certainly. The gentry always looked at her, but they saw her as a disgusting bug that might bite if it crawled too close.

She'd *needed* his respect. Now, she'd earned it. Along with a healthy dose of apprehension.

He hadn't seen his dreams when she'd touched him. She'd left him with nothing but his nightmares.

Rissa couldn't deny Rydekar had impressed her too. No one had managed to get out of her grasp until she'd allowed it before. Generally, she left her victim slobbering on the floor. Rydekar barely seemed winded.

He eyed her like she was a poisonous snake hiding under a bed of grass.

Good.

Rissa lifted her chin. "Never forget. I bite when I'm cornered."

A CROW'S NEST

Rissa retrieved a blue gown speckled with silver stars from the red and gold coffer at the foot of her bed, and pulled it over her chemise. It was backless, showing off the soft feathers growing at her back and on her shoulders.

As a child, she used to hide. She plucked feathers until her skin was red and blotched. She covered herself in long, heavy coats, even in the worst of summer's blaze. Now, she was unapologetically herself. Thorns, vines, feathers, and all. Concealing her nature hadn't earned her anything, save for discomfort and an extra dose of contempt from her peers. She liked backless gowns when the weather allowed it. Her feathers itched when constricted by fabric.

"How far are we going?" She'd never been to the Old Keep, but if she remembered her school days well enough, it was at the borders of the seelie and unseelie lands. That didn't mean much —the two fae lands adjoined for a hundred miles.

"The ride should take four hours or so."

Rissa stole a glance over her shoulder. Rydekar was touching her things, picking up a ring, a necklace, and throwing them back on her cabinets with an annoying carelessness.

No one else had ever touched her things like this. Not the maids who'd dusted her parlors, not her father, not her friends. It grated on her to watch him take trinket after trinket, analyzing them with his sharp violet eyes before setting them back down. Never had she felt so judged.

The thought of his living so very close to her was also unsettling. He should have been farther than a half-day's ride away. How was she ever going to feel safe again, knowing that he could get to her whenever he felt like it?

She shoved the anxiety back down. He wouldn't feel like it. He'd tracked her down because he was under the ridiculous misconception that she could help him unite the folk under one banner. Well, he was mistaken. Once she delivered the man who actually could do that, Rydekar Bane would never bother to think about her again.

"Where were you, before moving the court to the Old Keep?"

His amethyst eyes slid to hers. "Why do you ask?"

A pertinent question, to which she had no answer. None she'd voice. She would rather cut her tongue out than admit any curiosity or interest out loud. "This is called making conversation. You may have heard of it."

He turned back to her cabinet, picking up a black ring—the last piece of jewelry she'd made. "Here and there. The high court is set in White-croft, traditionally, but a monarch has to oversee all territories. The Old Keep is the only dwelling vast enough to comfortably house representatives from every one of my courts, as well as our army, and whoever consents to join us from Denarhelm. We'll remain there until the threat of Antheos is dealt with." Rydekar might exude power, but it was the first time he sounded like a gentry—courtly and callous all at once.

This was his professional facade, Rissa realized. She'd asked for casual conversation, and that was what she was getting.

She didn't like it much, so she let the subject drop.

Reluctantly, she threw a bloodred riding cloak over her shoulder. It wouldn't do to damage one of her prettier gowns on the ride south.

"You're fond of jewels." Rydekar said it as a fact, not a question, so she didn't bother to respond. "Like a crow picking up shiny things and bringing it to her nest."

Her eyes went to the sky, although she couldn't see it past her roof. Silently, she prayed the old gods to give her the strength not to murder the smug bastard. "Bird insults. That's so very original of you."

She'd been at the butt of a thousand of those, at the very least.

"If that's your idea of an insult, you need thicker skin to survive my court."

What she *needed* was a very sharp object to pierce his.

"These aren't fae-made," Rydekar noted. She didn't have to look to know which jewels he referred to. *Hers.* "Do you trade with dwarves?"

First she was a crow, and now a dwarf. Gritting her teeth, she resolved to remain silent.

Rydekar only sighed.

Rissa then rummaged inside each of her dozen coffers, until she'd found everything she was looking for. First, the clothes she used to train in as a girl; simple ranger gear, in browns and dark greens. They'd be ideal for her travels up north. She was glad that nostalgia—and fear that the chambermaids would finally throw them out—had pushed her to take them with her.

She stuffed whatever items looked useful to her in her red leather bag, pointedly ignoring Rydekar's inspection of everything she owned.

He touched her goblets, her silverware, her jewels, some of her gowns, walking around the treehouse like he belonged there. Like her haven was his domain.

Rissa made an inventory of her findings. A book detailing the use of wild plants, several elemental stones that came in handy for most spells, a healing salve, a filleting knife, a sewing kit, a pair of light velvet boots identical to the ones she was wearing. They were plain and flat, but spelled to keep her feet dry.

Looking around her circular room, she took in the hundreds of jewels, the few books she possessed, her journals—it had been years since she'd last written a word on them. None of it seemed useful for awakening a long-forgotten prince.

All her things would be here when she returned, waiting for her.

She swallowed a wave of nausea, ignoring the voice that whispered dark, foreboding notions. Of course she'd come back. She wasn't the first fae who'd ever traveled to the Wilderness. Her own father had wandered it several times.

"I'm ready."

Rydekar silently waved to the opening under the hatch, almost gallantly, inviting her to exit first.

He wasn't about to offer his back to her again. She'd truly managed to alter his opinion of her.

She grinned, victorious.

Rissa climbed down faster than she'd ascended, now that she'd made it clear the pushy king couldn't control her. She wasn't surprised to see him jump down past her, landing in an elegant crouch after the twelve-foot drop.

"Show off," she grumbled.

By the time she reached the ground, he was on his horse again, offering her his right hand to help her climb at his back, presumably.

Rissa stared at the extended palm in disbelief. He wore a ring that hadn't been on his middle finger moments ago. "That's mine," she pointed out.

"Is it, now?"

It most certainly was. It was the ring he'd touched earlier; her latest creation. She'd made it with a pretty red stone she'd found on a trek, bending a piece of blackened volcanic metal she'd picked up on the Fiery Peaks. The ring was too big for her, and she hadn't taken the time to adjust it. Now when she saw it, fitting perfectly on his finger, her stomach coiled uncomfortably. It looked like it belonged right there. Like it'd been made *for him*.

It hadn't. "Give it back."

"Why should I? You took something from me without asking. *You* should remember I always take payments for the debts owed to me."

That was payback for her retaliating against

his imperiousness. *Oh, the snake.* She was too furious to say a single word.

"Are you walking, or riding with me?"

Wordlessly, Rissa walked away from him. When she reached the tanned warrior, she lifted a hand to him. He snorted, but helped her up onto his horse.

The giant laughed as they trotted to join the rest of Rydekar's party, and Rissa couldn't tell whether he laughed *at* her or with her. "You're going to be tons of fun, I can tell." He glanced back at her. "Khalven Oberon."

"Nicely met. Rissa."

"I gathered, princess."

She could feel a grimace forming on her face. She'd never liked that title. Princesses were pretty, doted upon, and weak.

"Rissa's fine. You can leave the princess out."

"Rye might have a thing or two to say about that. He's a stickler for formality."

"It's rather fascinating that you seem to think I care about what *Rye* thinks."

His deep chuckle made his back vibrate in front of her. "All right, then. Let us behave like old friends. You can call me Khal. I'm the general of Tenebris's armies, and his highness's cousin."

That explained his familiarity with Rydekar. Rissa doubted many members of his court would have dared to make use of a nickname within earshot of the king.

"I thought I noticed a family resemblance. But I can't see the Lilwreath looks in you." The entire line of Lilwreaths was marked with amethyst blood, echoed either in the shade of their eyes or hair.

Khal nodded. "We're related on his mother's side. My parents rule in the Court of Ash—our court's relationship with the high crown has been tricky for generations, so Rydekar's father married my aunt to smooth things over."

"Ah! A political alliance." She grimaced in distaste. "How did that work out?"

"Well enough for the realm. Not so well for my aunt. Uncle Dorin, Rydekar's father, was never an easy man."

"I suppose the apple doesn't fall far from the tree."

Khal laughed goodheartedly. "Oh, in this case, it does. Difficult, they may be, but Rydekar is nothing like his father, thank the Old Gods."

Rissa might have asked what he meant, had Khal's steed not reached the head of the party, settling at Rydekar's right. One glance at his deadly glare, and she resolved to keep her mouth shut for now. She'd poked the bear enough for an hour or two.

"So, tell me, Khal. Anything I should know about the den of vipers I'm walking into?"

The general proceeded to gossip like an old hen, about this gentry and that, lower kings and queens. Rissa filed the names away in a corner of her mind as they trotted and galloped through the valleys, groves, and mountains separating the seelie lands from the unseelie kingdom of Tenebris.

FAIRY COURTS

L ike any child of the gentry, Rissa had traveled to various neighboring courts in her youth. She put a stop to it as soon as she was old enough to be heard. The Court of Sunlight might despise their nightmare of a princess, but out of respect, or perhaps fear, they had the decency to conceal most of their disgust. The insults were whispered behind her back, rarely said to her face. The youth of the Summer Court or the Bone Court adhered to no such edict.

She wasn't under any delusions. The unseelie realm would be much worse. Seelie were creatures of order and proprieties. Most nobles of Denarhelm would sooner eat their ears than be seen disobeying a rule. Unseelie thrived on chaos.

She would have thought that she'd feel something the moment they left the confines of her world for a realm so different, but the scenery never changed. Darkened woods, twisted olden trees with stories of their own. As the shadows shortened and the night turned red in the east, Rissa fell silent and too still. They must be close now.

"Are we still on seelie land?"

Khal glanced back over his shoulder. "No, we left your home at the base of the last mountain."

Never mind the mountain, they'd left her home at the base of her tree, back in the Darker Woods.

"We're not quite in Tenebris, though. The first settlers meant this place to remain courtless, not unlike the Wilderness. This part of the Murkwoods is home to many a shy folk."

She'd learned all that, naturally. "The high unseelie court is settled in the keep. It might as well be. How did you achieve that, in any case? I believed the Old Keep remains closed unless it's opened up by both a seelie and unseelie monarch. Was that rumor?"

Khal was generally forthcoming with answers, but now, he turned to his cousin. The king had remained too close for her liking throughout the ride. He attempted no answer, pretending he couldn't feel both of their gazes set on him.

"No need for a monarch." The taciturn, pale

Sea Land warrior at Rydekar's left hadn't said a word to her in the last few hours. Rissa would have sworn he only spoke now to spare Rydekar. "So long as a seelie and unseelie fae walk in together, the Old Keep's amenable."

"And you have a seelie fae with you?" She shouldn't have been surprised.

Rissa knew at least of one seelie who spent a fair bit of time in Tenebris—the captain of her father's guard, Meda, had been one of them for centuries. Yet she was astounded all the same. There was a considerable difference between dallying with the occasional unseelie folk and opening the doors to the ancestral home of their kind. One was a harmless distraction. The other could be seen as treason.

Rydekar finally saw fit to join the conversation. "Siobhe's seelie."

Siobhe. She'd heard that name before, but Rissa couldn't quite recall where. She scanned through her memories of princesses and duchesses and children of the gentry, but they all blurred together in one pretty, horrific picture.

"His wife," Khal clarified.

Rissa's gaze snapped to the king.

Of course. She remembered now. An elegant lady with silver-white hair, stuck to his arm the entire evening when they'd met. She hadn't said a word to anyone, least of all Rissa. Her eyes had been pale and beautiful; her limbs, long and so frail a burst of wind could have blown her away.

"Former wife," Rydekar amended.

In front of her, Khal's chest shook with silent laughter. "She still lives at court, does she not?"

"We were bound through a contract for a specific duration. That time has passed. She remains at court because she wishes it and I allow it."

Khal made no comment, but a chuckle escaped his mouth.

"We've talked of scandalous gowns, musicians, duels, and secret lovers, but you said not a word about a high queen," Rissa chided.

Though she spoke to Khal, it was Rydekar who growled an answer. "There is no high queen."

Oh, she'd touched a sensitive subject. Biting her lower lip hard enough to draw blood to keep from smirking, she pushed her luck further. "I mean, if this wife of yours is still the head of your court, she might as well be."

"*Former* wife!" he snarled.

Rissa shrugged. "Does she sit at the head of the table? Do the lords and ladies bow to her whenever she graces them with her presence?" With a wicked grin, she pushed. "Does she occasionally warm the king's bed?"

"You take a keen interest in what occurs in my bed, Serissa."

Now, she laughed. "Like any man of power, I suppose you think of little else than your own satisfaction. A few hard pumps before sending the ladies on their way with pocketsful of diamonds, I'd wager."

In her time in her father's court, Rissa had bedded two nobles before deciding to keep her favors to lower-born folks, who were more likely to work for it.

A gust of wind was the only warning she got. The next instant, Rydekar's hand was clasped around her neck, her ring digging into her sensitive flesh. He clutched it, hard. Too hard to find her breath. His eyes stared into hers, their cold glint rivaling the light of the fading moon.

Then he crushed it, thumb pressing on her artery, his fingers digging into the back of her neck.

Fear. He wanted to see fear in her eyes. She gave him none of it. Just a challenge.

Rydekar let go. "Pray you never find out, child. I'd take pleasure in breaking you."

A reasonable woman would have let him win. Let him think he'd bullied her into submission this one time.

She snorted. "Oh, *Rye*. You wish you could."

She dug her heels in the flanks of Khal's horse, and they swept farther uphill, reaching the summit first.

That was where she saw it for the first time.

A valley waking with the sunrise, flights of birds a-singing over an endless silver lake, and beyond, a castle plucked right out of her dreams.

The ivy-infested, eight-towered black and white edifice reflected on the frozen surface of the lake seemed both untamed and refined—a forest in a castle, or a castle built around a forest. She couldn't tell which. She knew one thing, though. She hated Rydekar for having found it first. This place belonged to her, and she to it. Just the sight of it moved something in her prickly, hardened heart.

The Old Keep, they dared call it. It wasn't.

It was the Fairy Courts.

Rissa dismounted the horse wordlessly, her steps rushing her forward as if in a trance.

Fairies were creatures of flesh, bones, blood, and magic. Every part of her resonated, dancing, singing, and screaming at her to reach the shores sooner.

She had work to do there. The keep needed her. It wanted her.

She grimaced, feeling Rydekar approach. If he ruined this moment for her, she'd bathe in his blood, never mind the consequences.

"Beautiful, is it not?"

"No." It wasn't beautiful. Butterflies, ladies, and swords were beautiful. "It's powerful."

The king nodded, and kept watching in reverent silence.

Perhaps he wasn't that bad after all.

Then, he offered her a hand. She hesitated, expecting a trick.

"You'll get there faster on a horse."

He had a point. Reluctantly, she climbed up behind him.

The king took off at full speed, leaving his company far behind. Though they galloped to catch up, no beast was going to rival his impressive warhorse. The steed was fast as an arrow. Feeling the wind around her, Rissa couldn't help but smile. They reached the lake and took a long slender bridge, never slowing down.

"Isn't it too warm for the lake to be frozen still?" She had to shout to be heard.

"It's frozen year-round."

She frowned. That wasn't right. The keep had been strategically built at the center of the lake for a reason: protection. In the event of an attack, no army could hope to reach it without the bridge. As the keep was self-sufficient, the folk could withstand any invasion.

"It shouldn't be."

"No spell we attempted so much as melted a drop of water."

Rydekar was in dire need of better sorcerers.

Soon, they reached heavy gates held wide open. "The high king!" shouted men from the guard tower. The scream echoed again and again, till the sound faded in the distance.

No wonder Rydekar was so fond of himself.

He slowed his horse at the gate, where a well-dressed redheaded fae curtsied as deep as she could in heavy knight's armor. "Send word ahead," he ordered without a greeting. "I am escorting the seelie queen."

Rissa's jaw dropped.

Oh, he didn't.

FOES AND FOES

"I am no queen." When would he get that through that thick, overly smug, unfairly gorgeous head of his?

One hand holding the reins lightly, he expertly led them along the endless paved avenue. "Are you or are you not the grand-daughter of Mab, the only child of the line of Braer currently accounted for?" Rydekar was light and casual as ever, completely ignoring the fact that he'd thrown her to the wolves mere moments ago.

"Bloodlines don't mean a thing. I have not been crowned, therefore I am not a queen." Pretending otherwise was a good way to end up with a sharp blade between her shoulder blades.

His only reply was a derisive snort. The cad!

Appealing to the sense of propriety of the unseelie high king was pointless. She tried another angle. "Look, if you wish to get along with the seelie lords, you can't go around dismissing their power."

The fire of dawn had yet to win its daily fight with darkness, but folk swarmed into the avenue, stumbling and stifling yawns to greet their monarchs.

The crowd stank of all kinds of indulgence, vices sticking to their skins. They hardly looked ready for any activity more stimulating than crawling into bed. Rissa realized that like her, these folk favored the night.

Rydekar indulged his people with the occasional wave and nod, but their eyes were set on her. Rissa grimaced.

"I am entirely uninterested in thirteen useless little lords who can't keep their affairs in order." He didn't bother to whisper. "The seelie folk, the seelie army concern me. Both need and desire unity. Unity you're here to provide. Remember our deal, Serissa."

She was about to argue that no part of said agreement involved her claiming a title she didn't hold, but a drunken, tottering fool tripped over his own feet. His frame hit the ground with a hollow thud, a mere foot away from Rydekar's horse. Though he had the sense to bring his hands up to protect his face, one of his light green antlers chipped at the edge. Rissa winced on his behalf. That must have hurt.

The puck only had time to wobble to his feet and mutter the start of what sounded like an apology before Rissa felt a wave of power wash over her. It felt like a seduction—coaxing, cajoling—but having been at the receiving end of that particular spell, she knew it for what it was. Complete domination. She couldn't help a shiver. The puck's body rose in the air, and approached them, pulled by invisible strings. A look of absolute horror haunted his bulging eyes.

He tried to speak, but his words caught in his throat.

He was getting strangled. Rissa swallowed. She'd expected cruelty. She'd expected violence. From Rydekar, and from the rest of the court. This was one step beyond that. There was no true purpose in harming a drunken fool. Yet Rydekar's amethyst eyes remained fixed on him as he begged and cried as well as his empty lungs allowed.

"Enough!" Until then, she'd kept her arms behind her back, balanced on either side of the horse's flank, touching Rydekar as little as she could in their position, but she shook his shoulder to get his attention. "The boy learned his lesson."

Half a smile curved his cruel lip. "Am I teaching something?"

No, he wasn't. He was entertaining himself. Hurting a lowly puck because he could. And because he wanted to show *her* he was a brutal beast she shouldn't displease.

They were testing each other at every turn, pushing and pulling the cord of power to establish dominance over each other. Rissa supposed it was natural. The king was used to having his will obeyed without question, because of his magic as much as his position, and she didn't bow to anyone. But this was the line. Innocent bystanders weren't going to get in the middle of their pissing contest.

Rissa folded her legs under her butt, and once she was balanced on the horse's back, lifted her bust to reach Rydekar's height. She tilted her head to his neck. With a clearer view of his face, she could see him open his mouth. Before he could ask what she was doing, she darted her tongue out, licking the tip of his long, curved ear. Whatever kind of magic one used, concentration was key. She didn't know one fae who could have remained indifferent to that treatment.

The poor puck dropped to the ground again, harder this time. He definitely wasn't having a good day. At least he was still breathing. Rissa sensed him, but her eyes remained on the predator she'd just nettled.

"You dare?" He looked at her like she was a bug he meant to squash under his boot, disgust mingling with anger.

She grinned. "I said enough. I don't like repeating myself."

"You dismissed my authority. In public. I've killed for less."

"We've already established that you need me. If anyone does the killing, it won't be you." Before he fit a word in, she held her hand up. "Besides, let's not pretend this little show was for the puck's benefit. You were flexing your muscles. Only, you fail to understand that I can't be intimidated. I'm not afraid of you. You *will not* address me as a queen, or I'll walk out of here. It's that simple."

Amethyst was supposed to be a cold color. It shouldn't have been able to burn so brightly.

The horse resumed its leisurely stroll. Considering the matter closed, Rissa returned to her former position, ass on the saddleless back.

They walked in silence until they'd reached the palace. Up close, the immense structure was as intimidating as it was magnificent. Age didn't seem to have touched the bright polished stone, though moss and ivy had claimed it. Wide, open arches curved at every floor, no doubt allowing for stunning views of the sky. Yet the moment they entered, heat warmed her cold fingers. The place had been spelled to remain pleasant throughout the year.

The main courtyard was crawling with flamboyant folk of many stations. Tall, ethereal beauties in silk and gossamer, the tiniest of devas, buzzing like butterflies, imps with long, sharp twigs for fingers, and goblins covered in gold. They were an odd bunch—not just gentry, not even high fae. Chaotic, Rissa supposed.

In the shadows of the courtyard, close to a set of colossal iron gates, stood a gathering unlike the rest of the crowd in every aspect. Rissa only recognized one of them, but had she never encountered Lord Gaulder, she would still have known the eleven gray-clad, sober, somber men for what they were. A company of seelie folk. Three lords, a handful of knights and servants. They bore discrete sigils on their chests. A reddish-brown oak leaf on Gaulder's chest, for the Autumn Court he ruled, and a spiderweb on the man standing at his right. Spiders were the symbol of the Kraver, head of the Court of Bones.

Rissa wet her lips.

Rydekar's horse reached the center of the circular courtyard, the thick crowd giving way before him. As one, all folded as low as they could. Fabric pooled on the ground as the ladies curtsied, eyes downcast. The men practically hit their heads on the pavement in their eagerness to bow as deeply as they could.

This was nothing like the kind of honor Rissa's father received. The Court of Sunlight, though none too impressed with his choice of breeding partner, respected Titus Brear, but they didn't fold low enough to cause discomfort.

This wasn't respect. It was fear.

Rydekar dismounted, then lifted his hand without turning to her. Rissa was tempted to snub him. She could get down from a damn horse by herself. She knew better. This court was watching her from the corners of their eyes, each of her moves analyzed, dissected.

Rissa noted that the seelie folk didn't so much as incline their backs. Not to Rydekar, and not to her.

She wasn't the only one to notice. Rydekar's glare closed on them.

To distract him before he decided on another show of power, she took his gloved hand and let him wordlessly lead her to the gates. Three large steps elevated the entrance of the keep. They walked up—as though Rydekar's great height wasn't enough to ensure he stood above all— before the king deigned turn to his folk and gesture his authorization to stand.

Rissa couldn't help it. "You're a prick," she mumbled, barely moving her mouth.

"Then you and I should get along famously. Kin calls to kin." Rydekar was beyond mumbling.

Rissa felt her energy drain as they approached the iron gates before them. She couldn't make sense of why a fae keep would have such monstrous doors. Iron was lethal to the folk.

Naturally, Rydekar barely seemed to sweat.

With a sharp grind that set her teeth on edge, the gates oscillated.

"Someone should grease those things."

"I can get you a pot of fat if you're volunteering. I'll watch."

Rissa didn't dignify him with an answer. She wished she could get away with kicking the king's royal ass, but beyond the gates, there were more eyes probing for weakness.

The gathering was endless. Hundreds and hundreds of folk had rushed to this endless hall painted black, green, and white. The colors of Mab, the first and last queen who'd ruled both seelie and unseelie. Her intricate symbol was carved everywhere—on the heavy planks of wood supporting the ceiling, on the columns, alcoves, and checkered flooring. A *B*, within an *A*, within an *M*. Though not exactly subtle, the symbol was pretty enough.

"Anyone I should watch out for?" Rissa was glad she sounded indifferent.

Truth be told, with every step further into the keep, she felt more trapped, threatened. She was surrounded by potential enemies. As much as she'd loved the Old Keep at first glance, she would have preferred to be a thousand miles away if it meant avoiding these people. Their eyes. Their whispers.

Rydekar didn't hesitate. "Everyone."

Finally, they reached two doors, leading to

yet another hall. That one wasn't as crowded. Rissa stiffened, seeing exactly what she'd expected all along: the gentry. Perfect specimens of delicate fairy beauty and brutal high-born strength. Eyes filled with malice and mischief. Her stomach tightened, unsettled.

As much as Rissa missed her father, she was glad that he had gone wandering again. When he was home, she felt compelled to visit every other month, and bear the uneasiness each time. The feeling of not belonging, along with the clear knowledge that everyone around her delighted in finding innovative ways to make her suffer.

"Especially her."

Before Rissa could ask who he meant, the most stunning female she'd ever had the pleasure of seeing stepped into view. Flushed cheeks, pale hair, soft mouth, luminous eyes.

In her youth, Rissa hadn't quite taken the measure of Siobhe. Now she gazed upon every inch of her magnificence, draped in a gossamer gown, translucent in the morning light.

She walked right to them, the first to have approached them since the puck. As she fell into an elegant curtsy, Rissa grinned, imagining Rydekar treating his former wife in the same manner as the drunken commoner.

Wishful thinking.

Especially her. Rydekar didn't trust Siobhe— or at least, he didn't think Rissa should.

Rydekar glanced at her with the ghost of a smile. Rissa would have sworn he knew how she'd uncharitably amused herself. And he didn't seem to disapprove.

The lady rose before the king gestured permission.

"When I heard you were bringing a seelie queen to us, I had to see it with my own eyes." Her voice was as sweet, mellifluous, and beautiful as one would expect of her.

Rissa finally understood. She knew why Rydekar had persisted in throwing a title over her. It was a shield and a weapon. The only one that she possessed against the likes of Siobhe, and the great lords and ladies within these halls. The only one they'd respect and fear.

"Siobhe, you remember Serissa, Queen Mab's granddaughter." He wasn't talking of any throne or crown this time. Trust him to respect her wishes the one time she didn't want him to. "Rissa, you were perhaps too young to have noticed Siobhe when we met at your father's court."

"I was fifteen, hardly a cub." She managed a smile. "You're still beautiful as the dawn."

Siobhe was well-bred. She blushed, thanked Rissa, and batted her long lashes, before turning to Rydekar again, firmly intent on keeping his attention. "Do you recollect the Court of

Sunlight, Rye? It was a delight. Its king was the most gallant..."

Rydekar moved around the woman, not indulging her with a reply. "The queen and I have much to discuss, and little time to do so."

Rissa managed to hide her smile, and shrugged apologetically before following Rydekar. They rushed out of that chamber, finally reaching a tower, with a long, curved stairway leading up into the light and down into darkness.

"Beautiful as the dawn," he echoed derisively.

Rissa shrugged. "What? She is." She wouldn't have been able to form the words if Siobhe hadn't been the measure of the praise.

Rydekar started to climb the stairs in silence. They'd passed seven floors before he finally took a door into a dark corridor.

There were arches just as grand here, but they were covered by thick velvet curtains.

"I'm partial to darkness," he told her, somewhat unnecessarily.

"So I see. Are we in your quarters?"

"We're in the royal quarters. Mab used to have her own rooms at the heart of the keep. When she wed your grandfather, he stayed in another apartment on this floor. I suppose they liked their freedom. Then came her lover Ovleron, my ancestor, and she had another set of rooms arranged for him. Mab's rooms are sealed, but I use Ovleron's. You may take Alder's. I had them dusted and aired before setting out to find you."

"You were confident I'd return with you." She didn't like his assumption.

He shrugged, leading the way again. "You're here, are you not?"

Smug bastard.

"You should learn to keep your thoughts guarded. A royal can't afford an open mind."

"*You* should learn to stay out of my head," she countered. He was right, she had to work on shielding herself here. Another reason why she preferred the woods to the company of high fae.

Rydekar opened an ivory carved door and revealed a room that looked nothing like what she would have expected of Alder Braer, famous hunter and scholar. It had a feminine touch—a bed made of twisted vines, a door surrounded by crystal and mirrors. So many mirrors. Large, small, standing, wall- mounted, silver, oak, polished, or tinted.

"Seriously?"

Rydekar was indifferent. "If you remained here, you could arrange them to your liking. As things stand, they'll suit our purpose. Tomorrow, we'll greet the court together. You will clearly state your intention to travel north in order to rally allies, and that you trust me to manage the decisions until then. Afterward, you'll be outfitted, supplied, and assisted as well as I can arrange, and you may go."

So many commands. "Are you able to talk without giving an order?"

"Are you able to follow one?" he countered.

They stared at each other in the doorway, until the seconds stretched in uncomfortable silence.

Rydekar was too close. His distinctive scent all but surrounded her. She couldn't bring herself to move away. She couldn't be the first to look away.

And she wasn't. Finally, he took a step back and turned on his heels. "Sleep."

Another order.

She made a rude gesture behind his back, sticking her tongue out for good measure.

"And grow up, while you're at it," he called out.

Somehow, he'd sensed her childish antics. She wasn't even a little bit sorry. The bastard deserved it.

THE KING'S MASK

Rydekar couldn't even begin to explain to himself why moving away from the door where he left the infuriating girl was so hard. She was purposely grating his nerves, infuriating him, testing him, teasing him like no one else dared. The girl needed serious spanking. But he knew what said spanking would lead to, and he had neither the time nor the inclination.

His little cousin was on her way north, and she wouldn't be coming back. Whether it be the wildlings of the dragons, the courtless shy folk, the army marching through the seelie land, or any other potential enemy, she was marching to her doom, and gleefully so.

Stop her. Keep her here. Protect her.

He would have given in to those instincts in another time—another life—but Rydekar had a long set of priorities in perfect order. First came his people, then this country, and finally his family. Everything else, including his own satisfaction, was far down the list. Rissa wasn't an item he could afford to add to it. Not even as an addendum. She was no one to him. She had to remain so.

Instead of heading to bed, as he would prefer at this early hour, Rydekar made his way to the floor right below the royal apartments. Two sets of light-footed steps joined his by the time he reached the painted hall leading to his personal study. "You like the girl."

Rydekar just snorted, refusing to gratify Khal's assumption with an answer.

"Come on, you can't fool me. I've seen the way you look at her. Like she's *interesting*. Like she exists."

Rydekar couldn't deny that he had a tendency to gaze through the fog of people surrounding him. They were of little consequence to him, until they either entertained or challenged him. Rissa...she'd done both before she spoke a single word. Damn Khal for noticing.

"If you'd ever looked at your wife like that, you'd still be married."

"Khal, for the love of all that's holy, stop winding him up." Havryll wasn't one to share his words, but when he spoke, people paid attention. Even Khal, who rarely even bothered to listen to what Rydekar had to say, always took notice of Havryll.

"Tell me you didn't see it," Rydekar's hotheaded cousin persisted. "Tell me Rye wasn't salivating over Serissa like a hunter over prey."

Rydekar's jaw tightened in annoyance, but at himself as much as Khal. He thought he'd been fairly good at hiding his attraction. Apparently not. He wondered whether Rissa had noticed it too. The possibility didn't sit well with him. Knowing just how much he wanted her would give her power over him. A power she'd be quick to use.

Thinking back to the way the chit had clasped her lips on his ear to disrupt his focus earlier, his fist tightened. Soft, electrifying lips that smelled of spring and sin. If they'd been alone, if he'd had an hour to spread her out, if she'd been anyone else, he would have taken her there and then, feasting on her flesh until she screamed.

But they hadn't been alone, he hadn't had an hour, and she was Serissa Braer.

Rissa may not have tuned into his reaction yet, in any case. Anyone kissing the sensitive curve of his ear unexpectedly would have succeeded in weakening his concentration. Perhaps Khal simply knew him too well.

They'd been raised together within the halls of the high court. Khal was two years Rydekar's senior, a fact that as a child, he had reminded him of quite often. The lone heir to the high throne of Tenebris, Rydekar had been protected by several knights everywhere he went, to his acute annoyance.

Khal was a third son, a superfluous boy no one quite knew what to do with. He was sent to Rye to be the future king's default friend, an automatically loyal follower based on bloodline. Rydekar had hated the very thought of having his friends chosen for him, and Khal had felt quite put out having to leave his life behind to follow his little cousin around. They'd been a disaster, fighting at the slightest provocation for years. Then when Rydekar was twelve, assassins came for him. Khal put himself in the path of danger to save his cousin. All of a sudden, without notice, although he was barely entering puberty, Rydekar felt power surge within him, and was able to stop his enemies in their tracks, controlling their minds and bodies. Khal and Rydekar stopped fighting each other, and started to fight the rest of the world instead.

Havryll joined them much later. The Sea Land courts were practically another world, not entirely part of the fae territory, but occasionally they traded or negotiated deals with the unseelie realm. Rydekar's great-great aunt was queen in one of the undersea kingdoms. While mysterious and highly private about their affairs, the Sea

Land were an ally of sorts. Still, seeing a sea fae prince turn up at the gates of the palace the high court occupied at the time, Whitecroft, hadn't been expected.

Havryll never explained what pushed him to leave his realm. He wasn't banished; Aunt Cissa provided a perfectly warm letter of introduction recommending him. Rydekar never asked. What mattered was that he had gained a ruthless, well-read, cunning advisor, and a friend with whom he could spar without worrying about knocking his head off at the first blow. They'd known each other for less than a decade, so naturally, he couldn't quite trust Havryll's loyalty yet, but he trusted his judgment, which was the next best thing.

Havryll didn't come alone. One of Rydekar's favorite fae had burst into his life at the same time as the mysterious prince. Seeing her enter the opposite end of the hall, running as fast as her little feet could carry her, he broke into a smile.

"If it isn't my favorite girl in the world!" Khal bellowed, opening his arms.

The child giggled, but jumped to Rydekar's arms. He shot his annoying cousin a triumphant glance. A girl of sense, Nyla preferred Rydekar to him.

She had been a baby when she and Havryll had joined the unseelie court. Now, Nyla was in her nineth year. Perhaps too old to be carried like a child, but Rydekar would behead anyone who suggested he stop. "Aren't you supposed to be in bed, you troublesome wench?"

The child pouted. "But I can't sleep if Uncle Havryll and you two are out there, you know I can't!"

He pressed his lips to her forehead, smiling into her turquoise hair. Sea-green tresses, pale skin, and eyes the exact color of coral, she was fire and water rolled into one adorable, if slightly manipulative package.

Rydekar guessed that Havryll's defection from the Sea Lands had something to do with the little girl, but if in almost ten years his friend hadn't seen fit to bring it up, he would leave well enough alone. Some knowledge was dangerous, and the last thing he'd ever want would be to put this precious child in danger.

"I know the feeling. When I was your age, and my grandmother ruled, she and her husband Velanor often left the keep for some duties that seemed very dangerous to me. I never could sleep either."

"Queen Charlotte?" The little girl's face brightened at the mention of Rydekar's grandmother.

For some reason, Charlotte fascinated her. Perhaps because she had been the first queen to be born of a human, yet Charlotte was known as one of the most ruthless of rulers in his line, almost as insanely bloodthirsty as her own grandmother, Nevlaria Bane. Nyla loved stories that ended in fire and blood, and most of those about Charlotte did.

"Yes, Queen Charlotte." He let the girl get back to her feet. Nyla rushed to demand a kiss first from Khal, and then from Havryll.

After obliging, her uncle coaxed her into heading for bed. "We have a little work to finish off. I'll come to you after."

"And you'll tell me a story?" Her big fiery eyes were so very full of hope.

Rydekar knew the logical answer was no—it was far too late to think of anything but sleep. He also knew that not one of the three of them could resist the little monster, and she was fully aware of it. She played the doe eyes and pouty lips for all they were worth.

"I'll tell you a story," Havryll conceded. "But only if you're wrapped up in bed by the time we are done."

Victorious, she trotted off down the hall, joining the short, pale-green-skinned imp nurse waiting for her next to her guards. Nyla was a princess of a Sea Land court, and as such, would have warranted some degree of protection, but because the three most powerful men in the high unseelie court cared for her, she was treated like a jewel of Tenebris. Had Rydekar fathered any child, they would have been given the same number of guards.

"Someone is going to have to tell her that her favorite king has found a girl he likes." Khal flashed his trademark smirk. "You know Nyla intends to marry you when she comes of age."

Havryll sighed, and Rydekar grimaced. The very thought of wedding a child he had carried in his arms, cared for, protected, and sung to on lonely nights made him want to vomit.

It wasn't that she was too young for him—not exactly. Among the folk, age was of little consequence. In a hundred years, why would it matter that they were born three hundred years apart? But while he could very well marry a girl much younger than him, he'd never touch this child who was for all intents and purposes, their daughter. Khal, Havryll, and he had raised her, though none of them would have qualified as an experienced parent. Khal spoiled the kid rotten, Havryll made up rules and promptly taught Nyla how to break them—proving that he belonged right here in the unseelie court. From what Rydekar knew of the Sea Lands, they were mostly of seelie inclination.

For his part, Rydekar commissioned several tutors, ladies in waiting, and nannies to ensure that the child was cared for by someone who actually knew what to do about her.

Khal's favorite pastime was attempting to get

on Rydekar's nerves, mostly because it was generally nigh on impossible. What his cousin didn't realize was that for once, he might manage to cut through his control. Rissa had chipped his armor, and his cool demeanor was ready to crumble. Rydekar was coming undone, slowly but surely.

Control was important to him. He hated the feeling of losing it. But he recognized it and he knew just what to do about it.

He needed to fuck, or fight. Maybe both.

That would have to wait.

TRAITOR'S BLOOD

They finally reached his study. Inside, Morgan, the head of his spies and two of his advisors, Crane and Denos, were animatedly arguing. They fell silent the moment the door opened before them, as was generally the case when the trio entered any room. They were a sight; Rydekar and Khal both colossal by fae standards, and moving with the lethal grace of warriors. Of a more classical build, Havryll's soundless steps and cold, cutting gaze were no less minacious.

"Your Grace, Your Highnesses..."

Rydekar waved off their attempt at courtesies, cutting the obeisance short. "To hell with your bowing. Any news?"

Hesitation. They *had* news, that much was clear, but it wasn't good. None of them wanted to share it first.

"Do I have to repeat myself?" His voice was soft as velvet. Fear flashed in the eyes of the woman and the two men who knew better than to test his patience at the best of times.

Morgan stepped forward, clicking the backs of her heels and bowing her head in one gesture. "I'm not sure how to say it. I regret to announce that we have a confirmed sighting of your father, sire."

"Oh boy," Khal grumbled, wisely choosing to make his way to the wooden cabinet where Rydekar kept his liquor. "Wait a minute. We better be imbibing for this." He poured six drinks, before taking one in each of his hands.

Khal joined Rydekar and raised the cups, wordlessly inviting him to choose one. Indifferent, Rydekar vaguely pointed his chin toward the left one.

He was suspicious of almost everyone, with good reasons. Not Khal though. If that drink was poisoned, it was the cup, or the alcohol itself that had been tampered with. Khal had risked his own life dozens of times for Rydekar. In exchange, Rydekar offered him something he bestowed upon no one else: his blind, unfailing trust.

Khal took a sip of both drinks before handing one to him. Rydekar frowned. He didn't like Khal using himself as a tester, and Khal knew it.

Most poisons couldn't take the life of a high-born fae, but Rydekar's bloodline was considerably muddled—with a colorful heritage that included human, pixie, and puck blood. Most of the time, it was a good thing. For one, his family was more prolific than most fae. Human blood had strengthened their seed. He was also faster, thanks to the swiftness of the pixies. And Rydekar was blessed with magic beyond the wildest imagination of most gentry. On the flip side, he could be poisoned. Not killed, perhaps, but certainly weakened.

Khal had a human grandfather—he'd feel the effects of a toxin faster than Rye. Rydekar still disliked his cousin's zeal.

The other four served themselves, rightfully not expecting the general of Tenebris's armies to attend to anyone but the high king.

Morgan downed her entire glass in one go. She was looking everywhere except at him, though Rydekar knew his spy was no coward. Whatever her awkwardness was about, it was terrible news for the realm, which meant that he had to hear it—now.

She bit her lower lip, a move that would have captured his attention in the past.

Morgan was a beautiful air folk, a winged fae of dainty limbs and rapid, graceful movements. Her nature made her the perfect spy, silent and swift when she needed to be, but also capable of infiltrating whatever court she wished to enter. Rydekar wasn't one to mix the affairs of the realm with his pleasures, but there was a time or two he had been tempted to make an exception for Morgan Vayra. Now, her sensual lips seemed too thin, too pink. His mind was on another mouth— darker, plumper.

He circled his desk and sat upon his imposing seat.

They stood in an informal study, one he occupied only when he wished for privacy. When they woke in a few hours, he would have to address the entire council, the lower kings and queens of various unseelie courts, and the rest of the lords, including the pompous seelies who'd graced him with their presence. For now, he wanted to be informed of everything going on, so that he could take action on the urgent matters, and think upon what could be dealt with later in his sleep.

His *father*. Rydekar's jaw ticked.

Dorin Bane was a consistent thorn in his side. After having killed his elder sister Nebula, Dorin fully expected his mother Charlotte to name him heir to the realm. When the queen retired, choosing Rydekar as her successor, Dorin pronounced her mad, and raised a pitiful army of fanatics to claim Tenebris.

Dorin wasn't a bad strategist, and his skills at combat shouldn't be underestimated. Still, his insurrection was squashed like bugs. They were too few in number to manage to take the crown.

Charlotte's last act as ruling queen was to banish her son. Since then, Dorin had attempted to sneak back into Tenebris a number of times.

Hearing his name now could not be a coincidence. Rydekar took a sip of his drink and let the alcohol burn his throat on the way down. "Talk."

"He is with Antheos, sire. I saw him myself, when I was leading a flight over the northwest of Denarhelm to see the progression of the enemy through the seelie land."

Khal spewed a trail of curses, but Rydekar could only sigh. He couldn't even pretend to be shocked about this development. He was certainly surprised, but it made sense for Dorin to ally with the west. A selfish, self-centered, ill-tempered fool with no sense of loyalty to his own kind, Rydekar's father was the worst of the high fae. He took everything for granted, and when he didn't get what he wanted, he lashed out in anger, no matter who got hurt.

Dorin had always been an issue of minor consequence. He lacked supporters among the gentry, and worse, he'd lost the respect of most unseelie courts—not for attempting a coup, but for being so easily thwarted. That said, at the head of a foreign army, he could become a true problem. For one, Dorin knew the land. He knew the location of the Old Keep, as well as every castle and fortress in Tenebris.

"How do we feel about patricide in these parts?" Havryll wondered out loud.

"Indifferent," Rydekar shot back.

That much was true. His ancestor, Nevlaria, had killed her own mother for the good of the realm—and her mother hadn't been a treacherous, spineless bastard.

Havryll nodded, and exited the room without taking his leave. If he was commissioning assassins, Rydekar didn't need to know.

"What of the seelie?" Useful as the news of Dorin may be, he hadn't sent Morgan north on a mission to locate his father. The spies had been dispatched to see what was going on with Denarhelm. "Are they sending their forces to us?"

Rydekar had addressed his missives weeks ago, as soon as the threat from Antheos became real. In all this time, the seelie realm sent a fair few number of ambassadors to discuss treaties and potential alliances, but nothing concrete happened. Only in the last few days, since Antheos breached the western borders of Denarhelm, had he been contacted with promises of troops traveling to him. But they were just that, promises. He needed the soldiers *here*.

Morgan nodded. "Some are. I've seen movements from the Court of Bone, the Court of Stars, the Summer and Winter Courts, though I can't say they sent all of their army. They're sending their people with a portion of their troops, and posting soldiers on the paths Antheos is taking." Rydekar nodded. He'd expected as much, and that was exactly what he needed. "Nothing from the Court of Sunlight. They reinforced their own borders, though."

"Is that all?" Denarhelm was divided into thirteen courts. One for each season—autumn, winter, spring, and summer—one for night, one for day—or Sunlight, as it was called. Then there was a Court of Stars, one for blood, one for bone, one for iron, one for silver, crystal, and the most reclusive of all, the White Court. Too many. The country should never have been divided and taken by so many rulers. Rissa had been right in her assumption that the lower kings and queens wouldn't like bowing to her after a thousand years of independence.

But they'd taken that independence for granted. Their oath was to the high court, still. They would bow. He needed them to. They needed it too, if they wanted to survive the storm.

"I only traveled along the west coast," Morgan replied. "My best spies are due back any time with news of the rest of the land. I thought you might want to know about your father as fast as possible, so I rushed back." A fair assumption.

"Old Dorin is inconsequential," scoffed Crane, a fat goblin with sharp teeth often wet with blood. Though these days he sank his teeth into politics more than flesh, he was a redoubtable enemy, and a worthy advisor in times of war, hence why he stood in this room although Rydekar wasn't fond of the old man. "He knows nothing about the seelie world, and has never lived in the Old Keep. So long as Antheos remains north, he's useless. Besides, Antheos will betray him sooner or later. They want to take the fae land from the folk, not serve it to him on a platter."

"'We don't know what Antheos promised Dorin," Denos pointed out. "He may have joined them out of spite."

"Oh, they promised him a crown." Khal shrugged. "That's the only thing Dorin has ever cared for."

Rydekar nodded in agreement. That alliance would eventually implode. The question was, how could he benefit from it? He filed all the information in his mind. "Anything else?" His gaze swept the room, pausing on Crane, then Denos and Morgan. No one had anything left to say. "Then I will see you at dusk in the throne room."

Getting up, Rydekar caught himself observing the bright sunrise, though it hurt his eyes, used as they were to darkness.

He never planned to speak, but words escaped his mouth nonetheless. "The seelie queen is to be reckoned with. She could be a powerful ally, or a deadly enemy. Treat her as such."

There was a lot more he could say about Serissa Braer, but he left it at that, before marching to the door, Khal on his heels.

His cousin, naturally, couldn't keep his mouth shut. "Wasn't that cute? You're telling them to treat your girlfriend right."

Crack.

The last shred of control splintered. He was done with propriety, done with being kingly, and most of all, he was done with his cousin.

Rydekar spun on his heels and punched Khal, aiming for his perfect teeth to wipe his smug grin off him.

Khal blocked the blow, and chuckled as he did it. "All right, all right. I'll leave you be. Just a word of advice, cousin. I saw through you with ease. If you want your princess to survive, you know what to do."

He did.

Rydekar remained silent, and they parted ways at the stairs, to their respective apartments.

GIVE AND TAKE

Rissa woke to the faint chords of violin, flute, and harp coming from somewhere in her immediate surroundings, her first clue that she wasn't back in her tree house. Before she opened her eyes, every memory of the previous night—and early morning— rushed to her.

She groaned, falling back onto the mattress of the annoyingly comfortable bed.

She was in the Old Keep, surrounded by foreign folk, at *his* behest. Bloody Rydekar Bane. And worse yet, she was on her way to the Wilderness, in order to wake a prince who'd been cursed for so many centuries no one alive remembered him.

She almost felt foolish now. If Tharsen hadn't been awakened before, perhaps it couldn't be done. Perhaps she'd waste her time on her journey north. What then?

Then, she'd have to turn back with her tail between her legs, and admit to being wrong. With any luck, by then Rydekar would have found another way to unite the folk, and leave her alone.

She was surprised to find the crystal pool filled with a scented foamy liquid that looked too pale to be wholly natural. Never a coward, but rarely a fool, she dipped a toe in. Delightful warmth spread over her feet, untangling tension she hadn't even felt.

This spelled substance wasn't water, but if it had been good enough for Alder Braer, husband to the fairy queen Mab, it certainly was good enough for her. Rissa shed her chemise and walked into the pool, finding it deep enough to engulf her entirely, even while standing up. She could swim four yards from one end to the next. The pool could host an orgy. With a grimace, she admitted that it probably had at one point. High fae weren't known for their pudor.

She settled at one side, head thrown back as she enjoyed the calming embrace of the strange liquid, closing her eyes to avoid looking at the dozens of mirrors in front of her.

Alder must have been quite vain.

It was strange that she knew almost nothing about her grandfather—or her grandmother.

Titus had been a thoughtful father, overall. He'd allotted her more time than most kings would have wasted on a girl unfit to be his heir. For all that, he never spoke about his illustrious parents.

Her body tingled with an awareness she already could identify.

He was near.

"Have you ever heard of knocking?" she asked as the door silently opened in front of Rydekar.

She kept her eyes shut.

He ignored her jab. "Good, you're awake. The court is gathered in the throne hall. They're curious about you. I need your entrance to befit your rank."

Now, she did open her eyes. To glare. Whatever sharp words she might have thought of, she kept them to herself.

Rydekar was holding a dress that seemed to have been cut from a cloth made of night sky, smooth, soft, with a dark velvet backdrop against the brightest of stars—pure diamonds. Not the small kind either.

"Oh, give it here!" She extended her arms greedily.

The corner of his mouth lifted. "I thought you might like it, little crow."

Her second glare didn't have much heat.

To her annoyance, he set it on her bed rather than bringing it to her.

"We wouldn't want it to get wet."

She conceded his point.

"Shall I call a lady in waiting?"

"I'll manage," she replied, disinclined to put up with a stranger.

Rydekar paused, and she rolled her eyes. "What, do you doubt I can look resplendent without aid?"

He shrugged. "Siobhe needs a dozen ladies and several servants to get ready."

"I'm no Siobhe," she shot back.

Truth was, if they were at the Court of Sunlight, she would have called upon Cressa, the half-puck city girl she'd plucked out of the slums to elevate as her maid. Cressa had wanted to join Rissa in her retreat, but knowing that she intended to spend her time in a treehouse, she'd bid her old friend to remain at court.

"I suppose you aren't. Could you manage to get ready in an hour?"

"Come find me in half that."

His eyebrow lifted, but he said nothing, nodding before leaving her to it.

Rissa rushed out of the bath. Delightful as it was, it had nothing on the *dress*. To her surprise, her clean skin was also dry to the touch, and pleasantly perfumed, in a way that seemed to increase her natural scent, rather than over-whelm it with strange tones.

Up close, the dress was a marvel of stitching,

lace, and embroidery in white-gold threads. It ought to be displayed like a piece of art.

She noted the back, so low it might show the tail of her spine. The skirt pooled with a small train.

"Oh, Rydekar."

The seelie folk didn't use the term thank you easily. Thanks were an insult, implying that whoever doing them a favor had gone out of their way. Saying "thank you" for a gift was like insinuating that the person was so poor they must have spent a great deal of their coin on the present. Yet the words were practically at her lips. She was grateful for this gown. It seemed made for her. How had he procured it in so short a time?

While thanks weren't the done thing, the folk did believe in repaying favors—preferably with something even more consequential in order to push the favor back onto the original giver.

Rissa didn't have anything with her that would suffice to express her appreciation.

But she could do something Rydekar would take for what it was: gratitude.

First, she donned the gown, delighting in its softness, its ethereal beauty, then she worked on braiding her hair, her skilled hands flying through the dark waves till they were half loose, half crowning her head. In her red leather bag, she found the cosmetics she needed to enhance her complexion: silver powder she trailed along her cheekbones, the curve of her long ears, and at the tip of her nose, and dark plum balm for her eyelids and mouth, giving her a hooded gaze. That would have been enough, if she didn't owe the unseelie king. As she did, she moved to the head of Alder Braer's bed—also plastered with too many mirrors.

The headboard was carved in the shape of a beautiful winged fae with open arms. Someone, perhaps Alder himself, had discarded a red crown that hung crooked on the angel's brow. Rissa made a face, but she took it nonetheless.

It was nothing like Mab's crown—a small, thin diadem with a black heart. But it'd do. For a moment, she'd play the king's game.

Staring at one of the many mirrors, Rissa lowered the crown onto her head. To her surprise, it came to life the moment she dropped it on her head, turning a blue-green similar to the tone of her feathers, though the stone remained black. At least it was less of an eyesore.

There was a knock at the door. She rolled her eyes.

"I'm ready."

Was she?

THE KING'S WAGER

To assume that the unseelie high court was but another fae court, like any of the others she'd seen, had been short-sighted and naive.

The seelie valued order. Titus's court was organized in rows upon rows of gentry arranged by height and rank and beauty. Here, there was no order, no logic. Pucks danced around fountains of wine, along with imps, goblins, and gentries draped in gold.

The cavernous hall was packed to the brim. Woodland fae with antlers curving like branches toward the ceiling, tailed folks, and some half shifted into beast forms—the head of a horse, the behind of a donkey. Those kinds of folk existed in the seelie realm, but they would never have been invited to the royal courts.

At the center of the hall, a dais bearing two thrones had been erected. Rissa noted the particular position of that stage: none of the vast arched windows could catch a perfect view of it, thereby protecting its occupants from a stray arrow. Yet, from the platform, they could observe every entry and exit. It wasn't only a place chosen for a ruler; it was meant for a warrior.

One of the thrones was white, with a tall, arched back. Vines ran alongside it, as though attempting to break it. A few gold roses grew along the stems. The other one was low and bloodred, with a fine black marbling. Though it resembled a chaise more than a throne, the imposing bulk and its place of power distinguished it as the seat of a monarch.

Rydekar was lying back on the latter throne, appearing casual, relaxed. He wasn't. This was nothing like the man who'd laid down on her bed with his eyes closed. This was a predator, a lion letting his pride know he didn't fear any of them via indolence.

Ladies flocked to him, batting their long lashes, attempting to catch his attention, but Rydekar didn't so much as deign to glance their way. He spoke to Havryll, who stood to his right, and another fae dressed in regal attire. Far from being offended at the slight, the ladies never stopped fawning. Didn't they have any self-respect? Though in truth, Rissa couldn't pretend she didn't see the appeal. Of all the weapons in his arsenal, his beauty was perhaps the most insidious.

Though the night was young, and most of the crowd must have only just risen from their slumber, the scent of vice clogged the air, barely covered by heady perfumes. The mixture was overwhelming. Had the high windows not been wide open, Rissa would have thrown up.

Her hand tightened on Khal's arm. She'd been relieved to find the affable general, rather than his galling cousin, when she'd opened her bedroom. The fact that the man had knocked rather than barging in should have been an indication that she wasn't dealing with Rydekar. Now, she was even more so. If the unseelie king had been the one she'd clung on to for dear life, she wouldn't have heard the end of it. She could imagine Rydekar's knowing grin, and the veiled insults he would have whispered in her ear.

Khal simply placed a calming hand on top of hers and smiled down at her reassuringly.

She had but a minute to compose herself and observe the scene, till a short, almost neckless pukka cleared his throat and tapped the marbled floor with a heavy staff shaped like a scepter—or a mace. "Her Royal Highness, Serissa Braer," the page announced loud and clear. "General Khalven Oberon."

Rissa expected that the crowd's gaze focused

on her, but she wouldn't know. Rydekar's violet eyes cut through the crowd to light on her. The advisor she didn't know kept talking to him, but he lifted one hand, cutting him off, all the while openly staring at her.

This was nothing like the way he'd looked at her before—like she was a disappointment, something he wished he could crush. It wasn't even like the way he'd eyed her with suspicion after she'd given him a taste of what one got for messing with a nightmare. He was looking at her like she was the only woman in the room, the only one who mattered. He was looking at her with hunger. Desire.

Rydekar rose from his red throne slowly. Although it was possible that she was just under the impression his movements were slow, focused as she was on him. Then he smiled, extending his palm forward. Toward her.

Come to me.

Rissa wished she could snort. He was playing games with their audience, fooling the court into thinking he cared for her. What had he said? That he wanted to present a united front to her people and his. This was a step beyond that. He was treating her like his lover. His *queen*. She wanted to throttle him, wipe his fake grin off his face.

What else had she expected? Rydekar had

made no secret of his desire to control the seelie forces. Faking a relationship with her was a shortcut to that in his warped mind, she guessed.

Rissa forced a breath out before letting go of Khal's arm with marked reluctance. She'd only taken one step when the crowd rushed to part before her, leaving a clear path to the throne.

No one had ever done that for her. Not at her father's court, not anywhere.

Keeping her gaze high, she climbed the seven steps until she reached Rydekar. He took her hand and bowed over to press his lips against the back of it.

Her eyes widened as an electric jolt coursed through her, starting underneath his mouth and running along her every limb, only to settle at her core.

Rydekar grinned against her skin, lifting his eyes to her before straightening up. "You like looking down on me," he noted.

Damn her, but she did.

Rissa let him guide her to the white throne at his side. "This wasn't part of our deal," she pointed out.

She'd made her stance clear about what she thought of pretending to occupy this very throne before they'd even reached the Old Keep, but though he'd been quick to accept her conditions, he was pushing at every opportunity.

"Hmm. Alden's crown suits you, by the way."

She wasn't even going there. "I'm keeping the dress." She'd considered offering to pay for it, or handing it back, but after that show, she'd earned it.

"Fine. It wouldn't suit me, in any case."

She fought against a smile, and lost miserably. "How did you get it so fast? Did it belong to one of the ladies of the court?"

"In a way," Rydekar replied.

She grimaced at the thought of wearing a discarded frock of Siobhe's, or another one of his old lovers. But no matter. She loved it too much to bring herself to care.

He leaned to her ear. "Jealousy does wonders for your complexion, little crow. But sheathe your talons—it was a present from my great-grandfather to his human wife, Sophie. I thought you were about the same size."

"Are you insinuating I'm shaped like a mortal?" Rissa needled.

Rydekar glanced down to the deep sweetheart neckline of her dress and wordlessly stared for several seconds, before returning to her eyes. He simply lifted a brow.

He had a point. She did have curves most lissome fairy ladies didn't tend to possess, perhaps courtesy of her mother—she wouldn't know.

"You're a—"

"Bastard. We've already established that." Rydekar returned to his seat. Louder, he said, "Crane, you have the pleasure of standing in the presence of Serissa Braer. Rissa, Crane Vorfj. He's advised and fought for my family for several generations."

The goblin inclined as low as he could. "How do you do?"

She presented her hand, and he moved to kiss it. His slimy lips made her want to wipe herself on something. As her only option was the beautiful dress she wore, Rissa refrained.

"We're glad you've joined us. Might we expect more seelie folk to travel to the Old Keep soon?"

Rydekar spared her the need of answering. "Several are on their way, and Rissa will travel north to gather our allies shortly." She just had to smile and nod, and the lord was pleased.

He excused himself shortly after, leaving them with only Havryll standing between both thrones.

Rissa observed the court tending to their machinations—gossiping, stealing glances at the dais, drinking, kissing in dark corners. "They don't seem concerned with their king's presence."

"So long as Havryll's here, they'll assume I'm occupied with grand affairs. When he leaves, I'll have to put up with supplicants." His mouth curved into a smile. "Or I suppose we'll have to, tonight, little crow."

"It won't work," she sniffed. "Pretending I'm yours. Most will see through the farce, but even if they don't, the seelie folk won't respect you more because of it."

"It's already working," Rydekar purred. His gaze trailed to a corner of the room she hadn't spotted yet.

The seelie lords she'd seen before were gathered there, every bit of their attention pinned on the dais.

Some seemed concerned, others, downright furious.

"Yesterday, you were no one. Today, with the might of my power, and your bloodline, they know they don't have any choice but to kneel."

Rissa shook her head.

Rydekar reached out, snatching her hand from her lap, and clasped it inside his grasp. Then, he kissed their intertwined fingers. "Shall we make a wager?"

Only a fool would gamble with a cunning fae king, but backing out would make her a coward. "State the terms," she replied noncommittally.

He tilted his head. "Dance with me."

Rissa's heart skipped a beat. Though she was fully aware that every bit of his attention was intended for the sake of the sea of courtiers, it wasn't every day Rydekar Bane set out to seduce the likes of her. She wasn't equipped to deal with him. Not without sustaining damage.

"That doesn't sound like much of a wager."

"Dance with me," he repeated. "And watch the seelie lords trip over themselves to cover you in blandishments, in their eagerness to win your favor."

Now she snorted.

Right.

"Just as soon as a pair of wings grow out of your horse's arse."

"If you're certain, then let us play this game. When I win, you'll do as I say for the rest of the night without a word of protest."

"And if I win?"

He waved his hand, unconcerned. "Claim whatever prize your heart may desire."

In short, he was utterly certain of himself. Which showed just how little he knew of seelie lords.

What did Rissa want of Rydekar? The thought that flashed in her mind set her cheeks on fire.

"Now that's interesting."

She gritted her teeth. "Stay out of my mind."

"Make me."

She snatched her hand back, and Rydekar chuckled. "Then it's settled. If you win, I'll kneel at your feet, spread your legs, and feast upon you until you scream my name."

"I'll pass. You can *just* kneel. In public," she added, intuiting just how painful that would be for him.

He shrugged. "You should ask for my throne while you're at it. You won't win."

They'd see.

THE GOLD OF VOLDERAS

A jolt of energy traveled south the moment he took her hand. Rissa's skin was too soft, too warm under his fingertips. Ignoring it, Rydekar guided her through the vast circular room.

He inclined his head slightly as dresses kissed the floor and knees were sharply bent. Though they bowed to him, the court's eyes were on his radiant partner, full of wonder and mischief.

She was a delight, perfectly mysterious, powerful, and with a name to match the high king's legacy. In another world, she might have had a true place here by his side, his hand on the small of her back, brushing her feathers like he had a right to.

Rydekar only had to lift one hand—the bows and strings interrupted their chamber music to launch into a jig, to the delight of his subjects.

Lords and urchins started to clap in time with the violins.

Detaching herself from him, Rissa stepped out of his grasp, to his annoyance. Then she plunged into the deepest of curtsies, and the clear view of her deep neckline cured him of any ire. No high fae should boast curves like hers.

She rose in one fluid motion, placing her left hand at her heart, and lifting the right in an impeccable posture. Then she danced. She danced like she was alone in the world, and didn't care for the eyes on her. She danced like she was a goddess and he, an unworthy mendicant. He should have known she wouldn't let him lead. *The brat.*

Shaking his head, more amused than put out, he stepped into her space with the aplomb of someone who didn't doubt he belonged there, and took her hand. She was agile and confident on her own—a well-bred fairy princess—but with him? She was wild, jumping in the air, pirouetting to get away. As she twirled, he slid his arm around her waist, wordlessly taking control. He felt it when she gave in, when she accepted his hands, his control. Rydekar kept her flush against his chest, heart beating against hers in a rhythm too erratic.

"Do you truly think that you're going to convince anyone with this act?" she whispered low—yet too loud in a room full of fair folk.

At least she had the sense to avoid airing the whole of their business in public.

"Everything doesn't have to be a battle, Serissa. Some things are rather simple." Yet as the words crossed his lips, he knew that this, his touching her, embracing her, was far from simple.

He was drawn to her like a moth to flame, but she'd burn him given half a chance, and he was sending her to her death.

Allowing her to run toward her death, specifically. Was there any difference, though?

She snorted, calling him out of his nonsensical musings.

"Isn't anyone going to join us?" she wondered, glancing at the crowd, stuck together against walls to leave a large circle clear at the center of the hall.

"Not unless I allow it."

"What a charmed life you must lead. No one treading on your toes without your consent."

"No one?" he repeated, lifting one brow.

Rissa's smiles were few and far between; the one or two times he'd seen her lips curve upward, he'd been fairly certain she was daydreaming about strangling him to death. Now, her face lit up, morphing into a softer, innocent monkey grin. Dimples appeared on either side of her high cheeks.

Dimples.

"I suppose fate thought fit to place me on

your path to manage that overinflated ego of yours."

She had *no* idea.

"Do you have human blood?" he wondered.

She shook her head. "I doubt it. I don't know much about my mother, but she's from the Wilderness."

He nodded, though her maddening curves and those honest-to-god dimples suggested otherwise.

"Why do you ask?"

"I'm attempting to understand you." Mostly, failing.

"How's that going?"

The music started to fade in one last long note. Letting her go with reluctance, he ignored her question. "Remember our bet."

On that note, he turned to his subjects, walking through the courtiers and petitioners, greeting those he liked by name, stopping to make small talk.

His awareness never left her. Rydekar smirked as he saw the seelie lords—who usually remained close to the wall, a vantage point where they could better take in and criticize everything about his manner of ruling—approach her.

Part of him burned to join her, protect her from their manipulation, discern whatever ill intent they may have toward her. But she was their queen, whether she admitted it or not. She had to figure out how to survive her people on her own.

How was his understanding of her going, she'd wondered? Terribly. Each time he uncovered another layer, it shrouded her in more mystique. She was strong, yet reserved, brash and teasing one moment, biting her lip the next. She had a unique power coursing through her veins and seemed utterly disinterested in making use of it. Rissa seemed tamed, like a bird of prey who never learned to fly. Caged. Yet her talons were still sharp and her wings, strong.

She could have been everything.

She wasn't.

THE FAIRY CHILD

O *ne century ago*

R ydekar was loath to leave the Court of Myth so late in the winter, when surely his counsel would be needed, but no one said no to Queen Charlotte. His grandmother wanted him on seelie land, so on seelie land he went.

"I thought it was supposed to get colder as we travel north," Siobhe moaned. "My furs are too warm."

His wife was excellent at moaning. Needless to say, she didn't think to simply remove a layer of fur, quite content to complain instead.

Rydekar looked out the window, tuning her

out. Khal had more patience. "The Court of Myth is higher, set on hills. The Court of Sunlight might be farther north, but it's practically at sea level. Besides, the descendants of Mab rule it. They have sunlight magic—they're bound to use it to make their winters more tolerable. Shouldn't you know that? You're from here, aren't you?"

Siobhe snorted. "Hardly. Denarhelm isn't like Tenebris. Each court is vastly different, and I haven't concerned myself with the doings of the Braer. I don't think they have much magic, anyway."

Khal glanced to Rydekar and sighed.

Siobhe hadn't been Rydekar's choice any more than his winter destination. Being the grandson of the unseelie queen came with a set of rules and expectations. One of them was that he marry advantageously for the realm. Siobhe, a princess of the Iron Court, had come with a mountain of gold and diamonds—a dowry they'd needed to rebuild various courts after centuries of war. She was pleasant enough to look at, and richer than the other options presented to him at his hundred and fiftieth birthday, so he picked her. They signed a contract for a hundred years, as was often the case for political alliances. After putting up with her for sixty-five years, Rydekar firmly intended to choose his wife far differently next time. He might even date the next princess, to ensure he could stand being in the same room as her without being taken by a sudden need to poke his eyeballs with a fork.

"King Titus is Mab's own son—her third-born," Khal lectured patiently. "I would not underestimate him."

"Then why has he not claimed Denarhelm?" The spoiled princess shrugged. "It's his birthright. He must know he can't handle it."

In the distance, the sun palace appeared. It was a golden monstrosity with slim towers stretching up so high they seemed to touch the clouds. As they approached, the scent of roses hit Rydekar, overwhelming yet strangely agreeable.

He'd been put out with this expedition since he was ordered to go, but now, a strange excitement crept into his bones.

Darkness claimed the sky on the horizon. They'd planned on reaching Volderas—the city of sunlight—by nightfall, because unseelie folk thrived in darkness. He didn't want to reach the house of strangers when he was exhausted.

The sandy path gave way to paved streets. Still looking out the carriage window, Rydekar took in the rows of almost-identical houses, growing larger and higher as they traveled closer to the keep.

Boring. Everything, from the perfect lawns to the beige doors and plucked trees, deserved a degree of contempt. Nature had no place in this land. It had been tamed, structured.

Rydekar had to admit that he sometimes felt exasperated with the way of the unseelie folk, who rarely saw a rule they weren't inclined to ignore, but the sheer perfection of this bland, grayish world made him crave a degree of freedom. A touch of color. One branch out of place.

The horses slowed at the gates; after his driver exchanged a few words with the guards, they swept right to the entrance of the palace— colossal, hideous doors painted white with curved columns supporting their weight.

One night. He only had to put up with this place for one night.

He stepped out of the carriage, a hand automatically sliding upward to assist Siobhe's descent. But his attention was on everything except his wife.

There was something about this impossibly insipid place—something that had caught and was retaining his notice. A scent, perhaps. Something warm and sweet underneath the roses.

Corridor after corridor, introduction after introduction, he grew more frustrated, needing to find whatever had claimed his curiosity. He wanted to look for it, like a wolf hunting fresh prey, but all eyes were on him.

Titus Braer was a tall, handsome man blessed with the mark of Mab, like Rydekar himself.

"Greetings, cousin." The king met him with all the civilities.

Rydekar wanted nothing more than to snub him and investigate.

"I'm here with the goodwill of Queen Charlotte."

"And who would this be?" The king glanced at Siobhe.

Rydekar should have introduced his wife right then, but he couldn't. A scent hit his nostrils, a scent of apple and pine, with something sweeter. A floral undertone. It definitely wasn't roses. He turned moments before a girl— little more than a child—burst in, running barefoot, in a light blue gown, hair flying out of her braids.

She was color splashing over a blank canvas. A touch of chaos. A breeze in this stuffy hall.

No one hindered her path to the front of the room, till she reached the king's side.

For one wild moment, fury gripped Rydekar's bones as he saw her kneel at the king's feet. If she was the king's lover, he would murder him. He'd murder everyone in this room and drag her to safety.

"Father, please, tell Morath I don't need more etiquette lessons."

She was Titus's child.

Of course she was.

"I may die if I have to listen to her tell me one

more time what's expected of a *proper lady*." The last two words were flung like she could think of no greater insult.

And Rydekar smiled.

"I'll do no such thing, petal." The king smiled fondly. "Perhaps when you cease to run in half-dressed while I'm entertaining guests, we might discuss how such lessons are superfluous."

Only then did she turn her attention to them —to *him*.

Her lips parted as she took him in, and she never looked away, unmoving.

"Rydekar Bane, my daughter Serissa."

He bowed low to Serissa Braer, and never forgot her name.

~

Far to the west, in the mortal lands, humans had a saying. Never trust a fae. Rissa remembered reading about it somewhere. She used to believe that their animosity toward her kind was due to their proximity to the unseelie realms. The dark fae were known for mischief, wickedness, and cruelty.

Now she knew better. It was never wise to trust any fae. Her, most of all. While she couldn't lie, it was rare that a truth escaped her lips these days.

"We share your sorrow, friend," she said, her voice a clear, musical sound filling the entire hall.

She smiled down at the two males in front of her, a pixie and a salamander, both adorned in attire woven from forest leaves and fresh moss.

The rest of the court was watching them with contempt, snickering and whispering nasty things. The gentry had never been kind to the fairies, the lower class of fae. The trouble these two brought to her attention was beneath their notice, worthy of contempt.

The pixie lived in a tree that the salamander's newborns had burned to a crisp, and since then, their two families had quarreled.

Such lowly issues were never brought before the royal court when her father ruled over it. It was customary for the heir to replace the current king in his absence. She was supposed to learn to rule. But on days when Rissa was on duty, the advisors saw that she heard nothing of consequence.

She didn't mind. Rissa may sit on the white ash throne occasionally, with a wreath of flowers in her hair, but she knew one thing. The crown of sunlight would never be hers.

The gentry may look down upon the salamander and the pixie. But her, they truly hated. Their disgust was as plain as starlight.

"We will consider your position and get back

to you by nightfall. In the meantime, you will cease your warmongering."

A lie, but one she could voice easily enough. She'd already made her decision, and Rissa wasn't in the mood to hear the gentry mock her for it.

The pixie glared at the salamander. Great or small, no member of the court respected her.

"I will have your oath, or I will take no action."

Her voice remained even and unfeeling. Indifference was a skill she'd learned long ago. The fae usually responded to it.

The two fairies bobbed their heads.

"Aye. Till nightfall then."

Rissa nodded. "We'll meet beneath your tree. Next."

It was a long day. Sacrilegious behaviors on fairy raths, littering in a naiad's pond—apparently, some youths were indeed that stupid—a well-meaning brownie messing with a banshee's curse, and various garden fae cross about the spring flowers this year. They blamed the court for not celebrating the ancient festivals meant to replenish the lands of their magic.

They weren't wrong. Rissa had seen the change, just in her fifteen years. The winters were colder and lasted longer. Night was swallowing sunlight.

But there was little she could do about it. She

appeased them with kind nonsense, general enough that the words wouldn't choke her throat. Finally, the last complaint was heard, and she was free.

Rissa rose from her father's throne and crossed the hall of starlight, the largest room in the Flower Garden, with a high glass ceiling that allowed for a clear view of the sky, her eyes forward, unblinking. She walked at an easy pace, though she longed to rush out. She could barely breathe in this place. In any of the castles. Beneath any roof.

She was a child of the wild, in and out. The soft dusting of colorful feathers at the side of her neck, all over her shoulders, was a constant reminder of that.

Finally, she was out. Rissa rushed to her quarters, kicked off her fancy shoes, and dropped her high-collared white and gold dress to the floor, exchanging the court raiment for a pair of light brown breeches and a leather top reinforced around the heart with metal plates. She sheathed her two long knives on her belt, took her bow, and finally leaped out her window, jumping down to freedom.

Her bare feet served her better than any shoes in the spring. She'd have to find a new pair of leather boots before winter, as her last pair was so worn they had holes her toes peeked through.

The gardens of this palace were extensive,

and to the south, they merged with the woods of Lailan, a domain she had yet to fully explore. The court rarely settled in the Flower Garden for long.

The directions to the pixie's troublesome tree had been clear enough for her to find it with ease. It was a beautiful oak tree that had no doubt grown for decades. Though one of the large sinuous branches was burned black, the tree hadn't suffered for it. As she'd expected, the fairies had been fighting for their pride, or perhaps because fighting was a good way to interrupt the dull monotony of their long lives.

She had an hour or two before sunlight, and neither complainant was anywhere near.

Good. She didn't enjoy making a spectacle of herself.

Rissa placed her hand on the trunk and smiled.

She was a wild thing. When they murmured the words as she passed them by, the gentry meant it as an insult. But to her, it was beautiful. None of them could hear, sense, and feel nature as well as she. The high fae of the courts were all refinement, pampered, jeweled, and perfumed. They'd long ago lost their connection with the earth under their feet.

Not she. She was the daughter of a beast who lived in the deepest part of the darkest kingdom. A wildling.

"You're barely wounded. Just a little bruised. No less beautiful."

The tree was proud, she could feel it. It adored being flattered, like all creatures. Rissa grinned before sending through some of her energy, eyes closed.

"Let me help."

The tree accepted it. By the time she opened her eyes again, there were no more burns. It stood taller, with more branches.

She climbed up, to watch the world from a little higher.

This forest was still so pure. She wished she could remain here for a little longer. Another week, another month, perhaps a year. But her father would move the court back to the summer lodge as soon as the snow melted off the ground.

"Impressive."

She froze in place, recognizing that voice and feeling his sharp gaze fixed on her.

The man from last night—Rydekar Bane, the unseelie high prince.

Rissa had never met such a stunning man. Not in any court, not in any dream. He was a god among fairies, perfect beyond imagining. She couldn't even bear to look at him, certain he could read her fascination on her flushing skin.

It was only fitting that a man as gorgeous as he would be a prince—*the* unseelie prince, likely to inherit the throne after his grandmother and father had their turns.

Rissa didn't turn to face him. "That's actually just basic energy exchange. Most folk could do it."

They *could*, but it wasn't in the court fae's nature to give something without expecting anything in return.

"Many a great folk wouldn't have enough strength to share that much energy without keeling over," the prince pointed out.

She couldn't help it; her chest puffed with pride. She didn't hear praises often, and while she'd hate to admit it, she craved them, feeding on sweet nothings like a bee on a flower. Her few compliments came from her father, and they didn't count at all.

"Or enough youth, perhaps. In time, you'll learn to never give without cause."

She should have seen a jab coming. Finally, she hopped off her perch, meeting his gaze head on.

She hadn't imagined the brightness of his purple eyes. Or his sharp bone structure. The defined jaw. She hadn't imagined anything.

Rydekar Bane wasn't like the boys she was expected to dance with at revelries—the boys who only asked her because protocol dictated they must, and rushed to pinch her feathers when her father couldn't see it. He wasn't like any boy at all. All man, too manly for any fae, he felt like a dangerous creature to stand too near to.

Rissa found that she didn't mind a little danger after all.

"What makes you think I don't have a pertinent reason to heal the tree?" She didn't. He couldn't know that, right?

Smirking with a mixture of amusement and contempt, Rydekar looked around. "Where's the reward of your labor?"

"Right here," she shot back. "You're paying attention to me, a lowly fairy child. I'd wager that doesn't happen every day."

Rydekar laughed with unreserved exuberance, like someone who wasn't used to it. "Not every day," he conceded. "How old are you, then, fairy child?"

She sighed. "Fifteen." Too old to be a child, too young for everything else. The high folk with a dose of original fairy blood could live hundreds, if not thousands of years. Rissa, granddaughter of Mab, might live forever if no one stabbed her in her back some day. "How about you?"

"Over ten times that." Rydekar grimaced. Strange. Once they were past their twenty-first year, the official majority, the folk rarely seemed to care about age. The first hundredth year was considered a rite of passage, but after that, why would age matter? They ceased to grow older as soon as their body was at its strongest form. "Two hundred and fifteen next summer."

"I'm a summer child, too." She couldn't decide why she felt compelled to share that.

"Before or after the solstice?"

"On the solstice," she replied.

Her turn to wince. Solstice children were known to be impulsive, unreliable, indecisive. Legend said they always came in pairs, but Rissa had no twin. When she was younger, she used to imagine she had one—a boy—and that her mother had chosen to keep him with her in the Wilderness. Now she knew that nightmares rarely ever bore more than one child, and almost always found a way to get rid of it, giving it away, trading it, or leaving it in the care of humans as a changeling, if they were inclined.

"On the solstice." Rydekar shook his head, slightly. "I take my leave, Serissa. Until we meet again."

Would they meet again?

She waved, feeling a sense of loss she couldn't quite place as his steps led him farther and farther away.

"When?"

Rissa didn't decide to open her mouth, but the word was out and carried by the wind.

Glancing back over his shoulder, Rydekar smiled. "Not soon enough."

OUT OF CONTROL

Damn Rydekar to hell and back; he was right. The seelie nobles *did* come to her, and though she could tell it cost them, all of them were playing nice. Sharp teeth hidden and deadly claws sheathed, they bowed, kissed her hand, lavished her with sweet words almost devoid of insults. Rissa was too smart to trust their sincerity, but it was a nice change all the same.

"Lady Serissa. You may not recall, but we met at your father's court." Forcan Gaulder was a slender gentry of great stature. His auburn hair, brushed off his face, and his deep green eyes were the only hint of color on his person. His habit, his shoes, and his long face were cold and ranged from shades of limestone to gray. He was the very picture of a flawless seelie king.

"Met" was a gross exaggeration. She'd been

present when he'd visited, once, and he thoroughly ignored her then.

She only smiled.

"We did not expect to find you here. I understood you were on a personal retreat, like your father."

The probing accusation rolled off her back like water off her smooth feathers. "Hm." She tilted her head. "I seem to remember you had a wonderful bird of prey with you on our last meeting. Was it a hawk?"

The lower king's jaw ticked. He wasn't accustomed to being ignored, by the look of it. After a lengthy pause, he deigned to reply. "A gyrfalcon. They tend to live in the winter court. It migrated for the winter."

"Shame. I would have quite liked to see it." Her eyes slid to a fae standing close behind the king. "I don't often forget a face. Have I seen yours?"

He evoked a vague sense of familiarity, though she'd only mentioned it to dismiss Gaulder.

Unless she was mistaken, the fae was young —younger than she. Physically, there was little to differentiate him from the Autumn King, though he seemed to have a little more color—redder hair, brighter clothes that weren't quite as boring. These two had to be related. But unlike Gaulder's, his eyes didn't feel lifeless and calculating.

The boy inclined his head. "I had the pleasure of being trained by Meda, Your Grace. Where she went, I followed for twenty years. We've crossed paths, briefly."

And they'd mutually ignored each other, no doubt. She credited him for his honesty.

Rissa was well placed to know that training with Meda was an intensive course that allowed for no distractions. She'd been placed under the warrior's wing for one painful year. She could barely imagine twenty years of drills, runs, daylong watches and strategy classes.

"You survived that dragon for two decades?"

He grinned, and his entire face morphed, confirming her theory: he was young—and considerably more pleasant than any of the other seelie folk gathered here.

On impulse, she reached for his elbow, hooking her arm underneath it. "Walk with me. You must have the most fascinating tales."

And he did. Assassin hunts, tangles with pirates, and of course, days where he considered sliding a poisonous snake inside Meda's chamber. Thankfully, he hadn't—the pixie would have had the snake's head on a pike, right along with his.

A deep baritone interrupted their friendly chatter. "What do they call you?" A snarl more than words.

Ignoring Rydekar, who'd somehow ended up entering their space without her noticing his approach—she must have been too engrossed—Rissa turned to the autumn boy. "Right. I quite forgot to ask."

They exchanged a candid grin. "Understandable, in your haste to escape getting bored to tears by my father's conversation."

So, he was one of the potential heirs of the autumn court. A worthy ally, though he wouldn't be of consequence for years to come. Still, Rissa liked him—and she wasn't politically inclined enough to dismiss a potential friend simply because he wasn't useful quite yet.

"I'm Teoran Gaulder." He spoke to her, not Rydekar, which could only infuriate the unseelie king.

Rissa's grin broadened at the thought. Though it cost her, she forced herself to keep her attention solely on Teoran, ignoring the predator lying in wait.

"Serissa Braer." That wasn't news to anyone, and she felt silly saying it. "I do prefer Rissa, though."

"Rissa it is, then."

"*Serissa*, your attention, please." She could hardly keep from rolling her eyes.

Finally, she turned to Rydekar. "Do you have to ruin any fun I might find?"

His expression barely changed, but she did catch a slight tremor of his lip, and the way his eyes brightened.

She just couldn't help poking that bear.

"We have a breakfast to preside over and you have a trip to get ready for afterwards. If you wish to delay either for your *fun*, do let me know."

He didn't reiterate his threat to throw her over his shoulder and plant her where he wanted her, like he had in the treehouse, but the threat was heavily implied in his smooth, pleasant tone.

A smooth, pleasant Rydekar was more concerning than a crochety one.

She *had* promised to obey him, for tonight at least. "Fine. Let us dine. I'm quite hungry." The mere mention of food was enough for her stomach to come alive. The folk hungered for many a thing; food was only one of them. Remembering to eat when she was otherwise occupied wasn't always easy. Besides, no one had offered her a bite since her arrival—a failing in the rules of hospitality that would not have been tolerated on seelie land. The snub may be deliberate or not, but she didn't care to find out.

Rydekar placed his hand on the small of her back to lead her away. Too stunned to think for a moment, she let him. Awareness electrified her bare skin under his cold palm, awakening a different kind of hunger altogether.

She hated how out of control the unseelie king made her feel.

After a few steps, she thought to glance back. "You'll sit next to me, won't you, Teoran?"

His green eyes brightened. "With pleasure, my queen."

She managed not to grunt. Not him, too.

Rydekar led the way to an impossibly long white oak table that hadn't dominated half the room moments ago. The king pulled the lone chair at one head of the table, inviting her to take a seat. When she did so, he bent his head close to her ear, breath flirting with the curve of her neck. "Don't trust the boy."

She snapped her head to him, before realizing the move brought their lips so, so very close. Barely an inch apart.

Thoughts left her mind—along with the rightful dose of indignation that had just flared into her bones. Rissa had no idea whether a second passed, or an entire year. She was empty of anything but a red, raw need. She could inch into him, just a little.

Rydekar straightened up and walked away to the other end of the table, joining Khal and Havryll.

Her jaw tightened.

Her eyes lowered to the empty silver place setting in front of her, and she tuned out the crowd, tuned out Teoran, and everything else.

How could he affect her so? No one ever had. Desire was an itch that occasionally needed to be scratched, like hunger, like thirst, and the occasional piss. Not something so wild and free it felt like a breathing, living entity craving to burst out of her.

She should be able to control this. She should be able to control herself.

This must be his power—a form of magic she wasn't equipped against.

Breaking fast, at court, was a grand affair with several courses of delicacies and delicious wine that tasted like ash on her tongue. She ignored Rydekar. She laughed and made small talk with Teoran and another neighbor whose name she never bothered to ask. What was said, she couldn't begin to recall.

She was a mess, and it was all his fault.

Rydekar remained still and silent, only taking one bite of each dish.

And his eyes stayed on her. Cautioning. Cruel. Penetrating.

Fuck you.

The words didn't cross her lips, but she pushed them to him, purposely reaching out to his mind.

A smile curved his perfect mouth.

You wish.

She'd never been closer to murder.

Because he was right. Deep down, she did.

DROPS OF HEAVEN

The music barely drowned out the chatter of the eager court, who sat merrily breaking their daily fast while gorging on rumors and whispers. Eyes bounced from the unseelie king to Rissa, his perceived counterpart, sporadically jumping to the lady seated at the very center of the long table: Siobhe, who ate solemnly and silently. The excitement was palpable. Never mind the threat of war, the very real possibility that the fae lands would soon once again be drenched in blood. This was the only spectacle they cared about.

Rissa would have loved to deny them, to focus on the excellent fungus roulade seasoned with a rosemary mousse, but she couldn't help adding to the theatrics. She glared at Rydekar. He, in return, smirked, like he knew all her secrets.

"You're to leave the Keep, I hear?"

She forced her gaze to slide away from Rydekar and to him. "Yes, as soon as tomorrow. Tonight, if I can manage it."

She hated herself for it, but Rissa's eyes had a will of their own. She looked at *him* again.

And who could blame her for keeping her eyes on the most dangerous predator in the vicinity?

Rydekar gestured for some wine. Had he even touched his food?

She wasn't concerned about his lack of appetite. She *wasn't*.

"I'd be delighted to escort you, if you wish for the company."

Rissa's eyebrows rose a fraction. "That may not be advisable." She couldn't imagine taking a prince of the Autumn Court with her to the Wilderness. What if he was harmed? She could cause a rift between two of the most powerful seelie kingdoms.

"I'd consider it an honor." His grin broadened. "My father's company has exhausted all its charms in one season."

It happened so fast she wouldn't have sensed it if her entire awareness wasn't focusing on Rydekar. One moment, she was shooting daggers with her eyes, the next, she caught a shift, swift and skillful.

Someone had moved next to him. Too fast.

Too purposeful. She could hardly detect who it had been—one of his friends at the table, one of the servants fussing over their drinks and plates. Her eyes barely made sense of it.

Rissa's nose was more trustworthy.

In the distance, with hundreds of perfumed folk blocking her, she couldn't identify a singular scent.

She rose and straightened up. Gone were the pretenses of paying attention to anything else; all eyes set on her. After a moment of uncertainty, the rest of the court rose as one. Everyone but Rydekar.

She could only stand, feeling foolish.

Rydekar smirked knowingly, as if to congratulate her, *see? You're queen, whatever you say.*

She wasn't, but these people would believe any lie he served them.

Frustrated, she imitated a move she'd seen her father do a thousand times, lifting one imperious hand, and lowering it. The courtiers returned to their dinner.

Shoulders squared, head high, she walked the length of the table till she reached its smug, maddening, unfairly beautiful king.

She knew before she reached his side. Poison. The sweet and tangy scent irked her nose, standing out against the rest. Elvenbane was a mixture of iron powder and rowan berries, blended with essence of enchanted apple, a winter fruit as rare as it was delicious. The senses of the faeries rarely caught elvenbane, overcome by the smell and taste of the fruit.

Rowan shrubs had been burned from Tenebris and Denarhelm centuries ago to curb the use of elvenbane. Iron and enchanted apple essence couldn't be mixed homogenously without the sticky berry juice as a solvent. But a determined foe could purchase rowan berries from the mortal lands.

At first, Rissa couldn't make sense of why one would bother to poison *him*. Lethal against small folk, elvenbane wasn't truly harmful to a high fae. They might need a nap, and feel a little worse for wear for an hour or two. Why would anyone risk a painful death sentence to see the king inconvenienced for mere instants?

Then it hit her. Rydekar wasn't a full-fledged high fae in the strictest sense. His blood was mixed with so many things—pixies, humans, and who knew what else. He might suffer more than a few hours of discomfort.

Though they'd pretended to resume their conversations, the court still observed her, thirsty for gossip. The handful of gentry closest to Rydekar didn't even disguise their scrutiny, blatantly staring at her.

"Is my side of the hall more to your liking, Rissa dear?"

"Hardly." Now she was put on the spot, she

realized she couldn't tell him about the poison—
not here, with so many eyes and ears on them.

It would lead to the kind of talk a king
couldn't afford; her father never showed such
weakness, and Rydekar was considerably more
closed off than Titus Braer.

She attempted to reach his mind again, but
earlier, she'd been moved by pure fury. Now, she
felt no such thing. Just a rising alarm she couldn't
justify. She wanted to strangle him half the time.
What if he was murdered at his own table? It
shouldn't have been any of her business.

Damn it to all hell. She snatched his drink
and downed it all, delightful gulp after gulp, until
there was not a dreg left.

His eyes had remained bright and amused
until then, but they lost all warmth as they locked
in on his gold-rimmed black leather goblet.

"Your drink is far better than mine, however."
And it was. Though it was but a drop of it, the
enchanted apple had transformed the black wine
into a galvanizing affair that enlightened all her
senses.

Everything looked brighter, more beautiful.
She felt so very hot. Perhaps she should remove a
layer or two. Perhaps she should shed all her
clothing and jump into the icy lake.

She shook her head, willing herself to remain
sane and conscious. "Pleasant as this gathering is,
I do have a trip to plan." Her voice sounded all

wrong. A purr. A caress. An invitation. "Lords, ladies, Your Grace. I take my leave."

Leaving the goblet behind, she walked out as fast as she could without running. Hot flashes started to pulse under her skin.

Where was that damn tower again?

THE KING'S BED

Rydekar brought his spoon to his mouth in a mechanical movement, barely tasting a thing as the food crossed his lips. He repeated the slow, careful move again, though every ounce of his mind and body rebelled against it. He needed to get up and follow Rissa *now*. Something was wrong.

Khal's agitation was hardly helping matters. Rydekar's cousin had the sense to remain seated at the table, but he was trying to catch his eye, and kept glancing at the goblet Rissa had all but snatched from his grasp. He hadn't failed to notice the slight tremor in her finger when she drank it, or the alarm in her eyes. Reading the situation had been easy enough; someone had attempted to poison him. They'd dared, right here in the open. And they might just have gotten away with it, too. Rydekar's attention had been completely focused on Rissa.

The move reeked of haste and impulsiveness. Whoever was behind this assassination attempt was so desperate that they'd risked their life to take his.

It was someone in this very room. Someone who'd been close to him moments ago. Likely a servant—or a fae disguised as one.

Rydekar's desire to get to the bottom of this situation was second only to his need to maintain an appearance of normalcy, in the eye of the unseelie court. A high king could not show anything akin to weakness. Admitting that something bothered him, that someone could have taken his life, was no wiser than slicing his arm open in a pool of sharks.

Havryll lifted his goblet to his lips, though he rarely drank wine. "The seelie queen's to leave the Old Keep soon, I understand?"

Rydekar held his friend's gaze, eyes narrowing. His advisor was many things. A conversationalist wasn't one of them, and this sounded an awful lot like small talk.

"Soon enough," he replied, eating another spoonful of goulash.

"Isn't that inadvisable in time of war?" Rofrakan, a warrior as long as he was large, with callused claret skin and horns curving backward, was one of the last of the ifrit, an ancient breed of fire warriors who served the Court of Ash.

In a time when that court had dishonored the high unseelie crown, they'd vowed their loyalty to Rydekar's great-grandmother. Rofrakan was the chief of their regiment, and sat on Rydekar's council. His appetite for war was almost as endless as his love for petit fours.

"And if your land was under attack, pray tell, where would you be?" Rydekar asked lightly.

The ifrit stared at his king open-mouthed, half offended by the question. "At the front, naturally." He cleared his throat. "But my blood is far less valuable. She's the last of the seelie line, and has borne no descendants."

"What good are the descendants of a kingdom in ruins? Let us see that Denarhelm remains in fae hands. Then, we'll think of bearing heirs."

A few paces down the table, Denos coughed his drink up. Anyone in hearing range was either gaping or repeating his words to the next guest in a hushed whisper. It hadn't escaped Rydekar's notice that he'd made the making of seelie heirs seem like his concern.

This court was readily fooled, and easily entertained.

"If she's to leave us so soon, the queen may wish for your company, sire," Havryll tossed lightly, with feigned carelessness.

He was giving Rydekar what he needed: an excuse to give in to his desire to follow after Rissa.

Part of him wanted to resist, because that impulse was too overwhelming, like an instinct, a primal need. His mind raced, control battling against longing.

In the end, control won, as it always did. He shook his head, eating another spoonful of soup. "If she wished it, she would have asked for it."

He had to go to her, but it could wait. It would wait. He had a set of duties to perform. He hadn't even received any petitioners yet, and his council was to gather right after breakfast. Checking on Rissa's welfare was at the bottom of a very long list of obligations. Farther up was his need to hear what she had to say about the poison, so he'd have to see her soon. For the right reasons.

Khal snorted. "That shows what you know of women, cousin."

He didn't grace that jab with his notice.

At the bottom of the table, in the corner he hadn't glanced at since she'd left it, the boy she'd enjoyed speaking to rose to his feet, and bowed low, wordlessly taking his leave.

Then he ran out of the room.

Rydekar watched him follow Rissa's trail out the heavy doors.

His spoon stilled before his lips.

"Ah! It looks like the queen may not need you after all, Rye," Khal teased.

Rydekar pointedly spun to face his cousin and smiled, showing every single one of his teeth. "You've volunteered to play king for the rest of the night. Well done, Khalven." He slid the leather circlet he wore onto Khal's head, setting it at an angle. Getting to his feet, Rydekar addressed the court. "Bring your requests to His Royal Highness until I return."

Khal groaned. It was hardly the first time he'd delegated his duty, and each time, Khal abhorred it. The court brought trivial matters they'd never bother Rydekar with to Khal, begging him to intervene in petty squabbles and give the crown's money to the stupidest of ventures. It had been some time since Khal had last served as king; since they'd first heard the whispers of war, Rydekar had remained in charge. But if anything of note occurred, his advisors would have the sense to look for him. At least, if they valued their heads.

Leaving the weight of the crown behind, Rydekar exited the great hall mere moments after the autumn prince.

He didn't need to track him or Rissa far. They were in the first corridor. So pale her skin had taken on bluish tones, she leaned against a wall, head buried between her hands. The boy was attempting to get her to follow him. "—can take you to my quarters."

Rydekar snorted. "I think not."

He had the pleasure of seeing Rissa pale further, then painfully lift her head to stare at him. Her dark eyes had never been brighter, or more beautiful. In their depths, he saw hints of amethyst, reflected on her lips and at the tip of her feathers.

She struggled to stand properly, unwilling to show weakness in front of him.

Rydekar didn't like it one bit. She hadn't minded being vulnerable a moment ago with that boy.

"You're ridiculous. I've seen stronger knees on a fawn."

She narrowed her eyes. "Well, you're..."

They'd never know what insult she might have spewed. In a few steps, he reached her, then lifted her up, cocooned in his arms. She yelped.

"Rydekar, really—"

He ignored how well she fit against his chest. He ignored how much he liked her this close. He ignored every feeling and sensation, save for his utter contempt for the boy glaring at him. "You can go, now. I'll take care of the queen's needs."

The boy didn't move. "She's unwell. I'd like to see her settled."

Rydekar could admit he had guts. "She's settled. With me."

He looked at Rissa for confirmation. She glanced between them and sighed, closing her eyes. "I'll be fine, Teoran. Your concern is appreciated. The king will see I make it to my rooms."

The boy nodded tightly and started to step away, before hesitation stilled his progress. "I'd like to reiterate my offer to accompany you on your journey, Your Grace. The seelie queen ought to be escorted by lords of her own courts," he pointed out with some force.

Rissa chewed on her lip.

Teoran was right. Rydekar barely ever went anywhere alone. He fully expected Rissa to reject his offer, stubborn as she was, and for once, he was glad for her stubbornness.

"Propriety demands it," the seelie prince insisted. "If you'd like to pick another warrior, we can—"

"No, it's fine. You can come. I plan to leave at dawn, after a rest, if that's suitable for you."

He grinned, and nodded.

She'd said yes.

Jaw tight, Rydekar started to carry her down the hall, and up into the tower.

She said yes. To that boy. Rydekar was dumbfounded. He was entirely used to her rejecting sense, kicking and screaming.

"Who knew all it took for you to be compliant is a few drops of poison." Beneath his casual tone, his voice was ice.

Rissa sighed. "I don't know Denarhelm as well as I should. The Autumn Court is in the east, south of the Wilderness. Teoran's company will be useful—and I can leave him behind when we reach his home."

If she believed that enamored boy would let her go to the Wilderness alone, she was kidding herself.

"Hm." Rydekar hadn't failed to notice the child's interest, though he couldn't tell whether Teoran fancied himself in love with Rissa or with the crown that belonged to her.

He steered them back to the most pressing matter. "The poison. What was it?"

"Elvenbane."

Rydekar cursed under his breath. No wonder she was enfeebled. He'd seen men collapse after a slight drop.

Never mind what this drink might have done to *him*. The mortal blood in his veins was unpredictable.

"A woman of sense would have knocked it over, not drunk it."

"A woman of sense would have let you drink it," she rejoined.

He grinned. If she was well enough to snub him, she'd be fine.

When they reached the last floor, he walked past her room, and Queen Mab's. "Where are you going?"

Rydekar kicked Ovleron's doors open. In the fortnight since they'd settled here, he'd done little to make the room his own, but it suited him well enough. The floor and walls were smooth black marble, supported by bloodred columns. Overhead, the ceiling was magicked to reflect the open sky.

A bed that could fit a dozen lovers presided over the room from the center. He laid her down, head on his pillow. Rissa immediately sat up, bringing the covers to her chin.

Rydekar sighed. "Do you have to make everything hard? Lie down. Rest."

"Rest?" She made it sound like she'd never heard the word before. "Unlikely, here, with you."

Could she have rested with the boy? Probably.

"Someone ought to look after you. Elvenbane won't kill you, but it may make you hallucinate, lose sense of where you are, or throw up in your throat."

These were only some of its delightful side effects.

"Don't you have anything better to do?"

He did, and the very thought of having set his duties aside for this was enough to pique him.

Rydekar opened the buttons of his coat and shed the dark piece of clothing as she watched.

He removed layer after layer. When he lifted

his shirt over his head, she finally cracked. "What are you doing?"

He grinned down at her. "I barely had time to shut my eyes an hour." That much was true. What Rydekar didn't say was that he rarely ever slept longer than that. "Someone must care for you, and I need to relax."

"How are you going to ensure I'm not drowning in my vomit if you're sleeping?"

"Who said anything about sleeping?"

He lowered his leather breeches to the floor and stepped out of them. Rissa purposely kept her gaze on his eyes, to his amusement. She was too obstinate to look away, and far too intimidated to stare at his underpants.

He flopped on top of the covers, and crawled to the top of the bed until he could set his head on one of the many pillows.

"Are you going to lie down, or do I have to make you?" he asked lightly.

He liked the idea of making her. She shook her head and lowered herself under the covers, close enough for him to feel her heat, hear her heartbeats, and bask in her heady scent. It was stronger than before, colorful, and so irresistible. After a moment, he realized why it had changed in his mind. "You smell of winter fruit."

No wonder he wanted to take a bite.

"Well, you smell of winter," she retorted.

Then she bit her lower lip, regretting it immediately.

"Oh?" He'd never heard that one.

Rissa shrugged, unwilling to elaborate.

"You're like a dessert, or a freshly picked flower. All sweet." Rydekar wondered how long it'd take for her smell to fade from his pillows.

He also wondered what she tasted like.

Bringing her here had been a mistake. The best kind of mistake.

"Why do I smell like winter, Serissa?" And why had she blushed when she said it?

She hesitated. "The winters aren't very harsh in Volderas, but we do burn fires in the great halls. I remember my father coming home, removing his boots and letting the mud dry by the embers." Her smile was full of mischief again. "That's what you smell like. Warm mud."

He read what she wouldn't say perfectly. It wasn't the mud that had bothered her. It was that this specific memory had come to mind. Something that reminded her of a time when she'd been safe and comfortable, in her father's company.

Rydekar was bothered too, for a different reason.

"You love your father," was all he said.

Even if he hadn't remembered their very first meeting, the affection was evident from both of them when father and daughter had looked at each other. He'd heard it in her voice, and seen it in her eyes when she mentioned him.

"It's hard not to love Titus. He's fun, and honorable, and so confident he walks into any room and *owns* it." She envied that, he could tell.

"So do you," Rydekar told her. "As do I. We're the rulers of the world. We have power of life and death over our subjects. What we do shapes kingdoms."

"Speak for yourself."

"You're a queen, Serissa. Why deny it? Why fight against it?" He didn't understand.

"Even if your assumption that Denarhelm could kneel under one banner again is correct, what makes you think that they'd kneel to me? My father is alive."

"Your father is the king of the Court of Sunlight. He had a chance at the high crown, and he turned his back on it. He rejected it. You're next in line."

"What if I reject it?" she quipped.

Infuriating woman. "Then Denarhelm will fall. Have you seen the lords? There are barely three of them under one roof here, and they're squabbling over details, fighting to remain in control. One promises five thousand soldiers only if the others may deliver as much. Then they bid against each other, because they are under the illusion their kingdoms are theirs to rule. They need someone to order them to act." And that someone couldn't be him. At least, not while Rissa breathed.

"Tharsen will be able to do that," she stated.

That again? Rydekar could only sigh. "What makes you think that's a good idea?"

"He's a pureblood fae. He's old—he was already five hundred years of age when his curse struck, and it's been thousands of years. No seelie king will dare go against him. Me? I'm a half-nightmare."

She said it like her lineage was relevant. He could only blink and shake his head. "And I'm a quarter human, with puck blood, and a fair amount of pixie, too. What does it matter? I'm powerful."

In their world, that was what it came down to. Power. She had so much at her feathertips. Why couldn't she see that was enough?

"You're unseelie. You don't know how the seelie realm works."

"I know the fae respect power and nothing else."

They could butt heads on this until the end of time. Rissa blew a breath. "You're impossible."

He laughed. That was rich, coming from her. "I suppose in that, at least, we're matched."

Silence stretched, more comfortable than it should have been between two strangers. Rydekar kept his eyes on her, watching the bluish hue of her skin fade to its usual warm gold. A stray curl fell down her forehead. He wanted to push it away, but resisted. Having her so very close was the worst kind of compulsion.

"You may not find what you seek up north, Rissa."

She bristled. "You don't know that."

"I know more than you do. If you listen to nothing else I say, listen to this: there's no shame in being wrong, as long as you can learn from it. There's no shame in retreating to bounce back. There's no shame in growing."

A crease appeared in the smooth plane of her forehead, between her eyes. "That sounded...far less condescending than anything else you've said to me. Almost wise."

He shrugged. "I'm some two hundred years older than you, fairy child."

She grinned, like she remembered his calling her just that, so long ago. Before he wore a crown. Before she was old enough to know better.

It had been a simpler world.

She eventually faded, giving into sleep, and Rydekar remained by her side, unmoving, studying each of her features.

Too soon. Her smell would fade too soon. And so would she.

FAREWELL

She woke alone in Rydekar's bed, though his scent was still everywhere. Patting the pillow he'd laid on, she found it cold.

She sat up, stretching with a yawn. How long had she been asleep?

The sky on the ceiling had streaks of red and gold running through the darkness. Getting out of bed, she walked to the closest window. Almost dawn. Turning to the door, she spotted something she hadn't seen at first: her travel bag, at the foot of the bed.

Frowning, she went to inspect it. Inside, there was everything she'd packed, along with an assortment of potions—healing salves, sleeping draught, and more. She noted a bag of dry meat, cheeses, and breads, along with a hefty purse filled with gold coins.

She whistled. One could buy a castle with this fortune.

Next to the bag, her riding habits had been laundered and folded, along with an assortment of weapons. Her own daggers, but also a knife so sharp the blade glinted in the light, and a longsword grand enough to have a name.

She couldn't picture Rydekar folding her clothes. A servant must have set it down.

She dressed in haste, regretfully removing her dress. Rydekar had better save it for her. If he gave it to another woman in her absence, she was going to cut off all his hair in his sleep.

She made her way down the flights of stairs of the tower, jumping them two at a time. Once she reached the ground level, she set out to find Rydekar through the corridors leading back to the great hall.

"Rissa!"

She had a ready smile for Teoran. "Good day to you. Are you still determined to follow me north?"

She would be the last to admit it, but she was quite relieved to set out accompanied. A map might have helped, but a guide was more than welcome.

"An entire army wouldn't deter me. Are you ready? The king showed me the horses we're to take."

She bobbed her head. "I was just going to say goodbye and go."

Teoran winced. "Rydekar let me know he's occupied. I'm sure we can find him if you need him, but he told me we could go when you got up."

Every word felt like a slap. He wanted her to go like this, without a word?

Of course he did. He was a great, busy lord, with no concern for her. All he cared about was what she could bring him. Beyond that, she was no one to him.

It hadn't felt like it last night as he lay next to her. It hadn't felt like it when he looked at her or danced with her. But that was the simple, unadorned truth.

She felt foolish for falling for the illusion he'd wanted to cast on the court. He was playing the role of her lover because it suited his agenda, but Rydekar Bane didn't care about her at all.

"All right. Let's go, then."

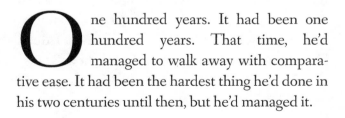

One hundred years. It had been one hundred years. That time, he'd managed to walk away with comparative ease. It had been the hardest thing he'd done in his two centuries until then, but he'd managed it.

Today? Watching her walk away from him, likely marching to her death, was worse. Haunting. Soul-destroying. But he bore it all the same.

"I should go with her." Khal shook his head. "Dammit, *you* should go with her."

Rydekar loosened his fists and walked away from the window overlooking the courtyard. One step. Another one. He reached the mantelpiece adorning his fireplace and leaned against it, willing himself to remain right there.

Still, he turned to the window, and kept looking.

The two riders were at the gates now.

Khal slammed his book shut and stared pointedly at him.

"I have a kingdom to rule. Two, in fact."

"She's likely to die out there. If not by Antheos's army, then by the hand of the wilderlings, or that seelie knight. And let's imagine that both spare her somehow. The cursed prince was a psychopath. You know it. I know it. The entire world knows it."

"Except for children who'd rather believe in fairy tales than in reality. She could have opened any book and worked it out. She's a liability. Impulsive, self-centered, with no sense of duty. She better serves us in the north than here."

"In the north, where she's likely to die?"

Rydekar lifted his chin.

"That's what you're saying, isn't it? That you

think she's better off dead. She poisoned herself for you!"

"She's a liability," he repeated steadily.

"No." Khal laughed. There was no humor to it, none of his usual cheeriness. "She's a vulnerability. *Yours.* Do you think me blind, cousin? I used to wonder why you were so adamant to dissolve your alliance with Siobhe. She's an idiot, but you put up with it for over half a century, then suddenly, you were set on breaking a contract—going back on your word. I always wondered. Then yesterday during your spectacle at court, I remembered. You met her at her father's court. You wanted to be free when she came of age."

Rydekar quite liked his cousin. More than anyone else in this court. All the same, he glanced at the dagger on his belt and considered practicing his throwing arm.

"But you didn't go to her. Not until now—when you needed help. You didn't go to find the seelie queen. You went in search of your mate."

Two moves. His finger pulled on the bejeweled pommel, chucking it in the air. Catching it, he flung it with speed and precision. The iron blade sliced his cousin's cheek before embedding itself in a painted hardwood wall.

"If you'd been anyone else and said those words to me, you'd be dead. Have a care."

Khal snorted. "Have a care? You're the one

throwing away what any other fae would be cherishing. Protecting. How can you?"

"I am the unseelie king." Those words were matter of fact. "You should know what it means. I have no weaknesses."

He couldn't afford any.

Rydekar didn't care for Rissa. She'd given him no reason to like her, thank the gods. But he fully comprehended that he could and would grow to adore her with ease. Another day. Another week. How long would it be before the good of his kingdom came second to him?

If she'd been what he needed, a true queen, he would have moved heaven and hell to tie her to him. As things stood, the best thing he could do for himself and his kingdom was to let her disappear.

Khal was speechless for a moment. Unfortunately, he recovered. "I always knew you were heartless. I never realized you were foolish."

On that note, Khal walked out of the room, slamming the doors on his way out.

Rydekar returned to the window. The pale horse and its rider were outside the keep, galloping over the bridge. His eyes narrowed on the knight on the brown steed to Rissa's side.

Rydekar managed a smile that didn't reach his eyes as he felt Nyla's approach. "What did we say about knocking before entering my study?"

The child ignored him. "Where is Uncle Khal going?"

Rydekar frowned.

"He said goodbye to me. I don't like when he's going away."

The child had serious abandonment issues.

"We had a disagreement. He'll be back shortly."

Rydekar was quite certain of himself, until his eyes caught a familiar figure rushing across the courtyard.

A page brought Khal his fastest horse. Mounting the beast, his cousin set off at full speed, charging out of the keep.

Rydekar kept watching. The horse he'd given Rissa was a stallion who might have been difficult for an inexperienced rider, but she managed him beautifully, and he'd serve her well. Khal's horse strained to join her, until she realized she was followed and slowed to meet him.

They exchanged a brief conversation, then all three riders resumed their ride together.

Rydekar couldn't make sense of his own feelings. Some betrayal, some amusement, a pinch of admiration. Khal had some guts to blatantly defy the will of his king.

It looked like Rissa had a second companion. One Rydekar did trust.

"You're smiling," Nyla noted.

"Am I?"

He was genuinely surprised to find that she was correct. He was overall quite pleased with the development.

Although he might have to kill Khal on his way back, all the same.

THE OTHER SIDE

Used as she was to the milder weather of Volderas and its surrounding lands, Rissa might have hated traveling in the cold of winter, but the crisp white touching her cheeks didn't bother her, and she loved the light of the sun over the snow-covered ground.

"By the old gods!" Khal didn't share her perspective. "It's colder than a witch's tit. And trust me, I've sucked one or two of those."

Teoran snorted. The autumn prince and the unseelie prince didn't seem to get along, though Rissa wondered whether they were purposely at odds simply based on their belonging to different courts.

They were on their second day's ride out of the Old Keep. At Khal's insistence, they were sticking to smaller, sinuous paths that led them away from towns, cities, and courts. Teoran disagreed with that decision, but he reluctantly led the way when Rissa supported the unseelie man's choice.

It wasn't Teoran's fault; he didn't know the true purpose of their voyage. Stopping at every lord's keep would have delayed her, and made their trip all the more unpleasant.

Khal only thought of their safety. He remained careful, watchful and confident in his ability to protect them from upcoming danger. Rissa couldn't deny that the two men's presence made the trip considerably more agreeable than her initial plan of traveling alone would have been.

For one, Khal knew how to cook. Rissa could roast a rabbit and pick enough berries to sustain herself in the wild, but in her years in the Darker Woods, she'd barely eaten anything else.

Teoran shot a pheasant on their first day, and with just a few roots and herbs, Khal turned it into a soup worthy of the royal cooks in the Old Keep.

They polished off what was left of it at high noon, cleaning up their wooden bowls with the last of the bread she'd packed.

"We should purchase some food when we next pass a village," Rissa suggested.

They could always hunt if necessary, but game was rare in winter. The bread and cheese had been valuable late at night.

Khal nodded slowly.

"Why not halt in Deanon?" Teoran frowned. "We're close enough."

Deanon housed the Court of Bones. To Teoran, stopping there was logical.

Rissa exchanged a look with Khal, and the seelie prince didn't miss it.

"I feel like I'm out of the loop here. Why are we avoiding every city, every royal court?"

She bit her lip.

"Are we not seeking allies?"

"Your queen has specific ideas about the ally she's looking for," Khal said, with something that sounded like disapproval.

He hadn't said a word against her quest until then. Rissa didn't like it. Rydekar's disapproval was a given, but she'd been under the impression Khal understood her better. Apparently not.

Teoran turned to her, staring pointedly, demanding an answer.

She swallowed. "I'd like to reach the forbidden mountain, and free Tharsen. It's but a four-day ride to the Wilderness, and then perhaps another day or two to reach the mountain. Then, we could return south together, gathering the courts on our way."

Why did she feel foolish laying out her plan right now? It was sensible enough. Rydekar's dismissal must have hit harder than she intended to let it.

Teoran's astonished stare certainly wasn't helping. At long last, he asked, "Whyever would you want to do that?"

Wasn't it obvious? "He can unite Denarhelm better than I ever could. None of the kings are likely to listen to *me*. They didn't respect me as a princess. They'll never obey me as queen."

Teoran snorted. "The great lords don't respect anyone but themselves, that's why they're lords. It doesn't change the fact that they're sworn to obey the high crown—and that you're next in line to inherit it."

Rissa shook her head.

"No, listen to me. As royals, we're never going to make anyone happy. It's not in our nature. Siblings will see us as potential rivals; our parents, as their replacement; our subjects, as tyrants. They want to crush us. If not our flesh, then at the very least, our spirits. I was dragged through mud, dropped down a well, and left to drown as a child. I pissed myself out of fear when my cousin abandoned me near a pack of wolves. I was seven."

Rissa gaped as she stared at the fae. Young, he may be, but he radiated confidence and strength. She couldn't picture any of what he'd just confessed.

"How did you kill them?" Khal asked. "The wolves."

Teoran rolled his eyes. "Straight to the killing. How boorish. I befriended them, you brute."

Khal snorted. "He's right, though. There's a reason my parents sent me to Rye as a child. My siblings didn't take kindly to a brother gifted with a blade. It was safer to get me out of the way—for me and them. As for Rye, he had to deal with his father, who tried to kill him at puberty just as soon as he started to grow into his powers."

Rissa was too shocked to say a word, barely capable of imagining it. As a teenager, she might have had to deal with bullying from gentry children, but her father had showered her with as much affection as Titus Braer was able to spare on anyone.

You love your father, Rydekar had told her, and he'd sounded a little surprised. As though, to him, fathers weren't entities one could love.

"I can't rule Denarhelm. Tharsen was raised for it. He knows how to—"

"Tharsen was banished by his own mother, for good reason," Teoran interrupted. "What I've read of him in my studies suggests he was selfish, and so power hungry he was happy to siphon the lives of his subjects to increase his own strength. The lords may kneel to him out of fear long enough to beat back Antheos, but then we'll be left with a true monster."

"That's a rumor," she said. "Ask the right

person, and every king is a tyrant, for demanding taxes or asking for soldiers or—"

"No other king is a *siphon*." Teoran shook his head. "I can't support this. And if he is," he pointed to Khal, "ask yourself why. With Tharsen at the head of Denarhelm, Tenebris can invade tomorrow. The kings will be only too happy to switch allegiances."

Khal rolled his eyes. "Don't look at me. I'm only here to make sure she makes it back in one piece."

"Rydekar didn't order you to come, then?" Teoran challenged.

"He didn't. And I didn't ask. I like Rissa; she's loyal and I believe she's exactly what the fae world needs, so I'm here to ensure she keeps her head on her shoulders. How about you, autumn boy? Can you say the same?"

Teoran's teeth flashed. "I'm here because until such a time as she rejects her crown, Serissa Braer is the high seelie queen. *My* queen." He turned to her. "You have been since you came of age. My father's council has discussed you every year since. Some advisors were in favor of coming to you of our own accord, others half whispered advice to hire assassins before you were too hard a target. In the end, my father opted to ignore you. I can guarantee the rest of the lower kings and queens had the exact same discussion in their courts, and they all chose clinging to their power a while longer. But they know you're queen. You only have to ask, and they will kneel."

She shook her head. "You live in another world."

In her reality, she was just Rissa, too wild for the courts, too pampered for the wild. Content to live in the woods like a hag.

"In that world, you rule. You can join it anytime."

She was too stunned to reply.

"Come to the Court of Bones with me. Let me prove it to you."

There was only one thing holding her back. She didn't want him to be right. She liked the comfort of her world. She liked her invisibility, her impotence. She wore her lack of concerns like a shroud, letting it warm her at night.

If he was right, then she had a role, a duty.

If he was right, she should be at the Old Keep, calling on the seelie forces and preparing for war right along with Rydekar.

Two men, so different in everything—age, affinity, taste, demeanor. Yet they both agreed about her place in the seelie dynasty.

Right at the top.

He couldn't be right. They couldn't be right.

Still, she owed it to herself to find out.

"All right. To Deanon, then."

CITY OF BONES

"What!" Rydekar roared.

The page who'd just entered the war room practically pissed himself, trembling like a leaf. "I—a message, my king. From the front. I was told to bring it straight to you. A thousand apologies, your great—"

Rydekar redirected his attention to the map of the fae lands—Tenebris to the south and Denarhelm in the north. His eyes hovered over the Wilderness. He'd given Rissa a fast horse, but he doubted she'd made it yet. If she'd ridden at high speed without a break, perhaps, but she wasn't one to kill her horse for a quest, vital as it may be.

"Give it here," Havryll said.

The page bit his lip. "I was told... Sir, the rider was clear. He said I was to give it to the king, no one else."

Rydekar's gaze slowly lifted from the map to the page. "Obey."

That one word was said with a compulsion strong enough to make a strong man fall to his knees. The page stuffed the parchment in Havryll's hand and ran out of the room.

"Was that necessary?" Havryll asked.

Rydekar shrugged. He knew his temper had seen better days.

"Anything of note?"

Havryll's eyes scanned the missive. He snorted, handing it to Rydekar.

He immediately identified the florid hand that had written it.

It has come to our notice that the king may feel forlorn, and in our capacity as the ladies of the keep, we'd like to extend our invitation to our private gathering...

Was she *serious?*

The words may be interpreted in different ways, but Rydekar knew Siobhe. She was inviting him to an orgy.

"She might have a point. You need to get laid."

Havryll wasn't entirely wrong. Rydekar needed a release. The problem was that the thought of bringing anyone to his bed was as appealing as the prospect of jumping in a river full of alligators.

At least, anyone here.

It had been three days since Rissa's departure and Rydekar ought to be delighted. The seelie lords here were finally paying attention to what he was saying. Missives had flown everywhere throughout Denarhelm since Rissa's departure, and his spies reported that the armies from the lower courts were moving south in great numbers, along with caravans of civilians. Like he'd suggested for months, all of the seelie courts also sent hundreds of soldiers to their western borders to create a wall beyond which their enemies couldn't easily penetrate. That move required a degree of trust and cohesion the thirteen courts hadn't seemed capable of. They did it all the same.

His plan was working. The seelie had moved at the first hint that their queen supported him.

If only she were here, where she belonged, all would be well.

Rydekar also missed Khal, though he loathed admitting it. His cousin was always at his side, a presence he'd grown to rely on so much he didn't pay attention to it half the time.

"When the lords come in an hour or so, you'll show them our progress and let them know we've moved to fortify the borders. I'll take the guard, and we'll be back in three to four days. I trust you can run things here."

His latest intel suggested the Antheosan army had progressed to Braon, in the White Court. That suggested they'd travel through four of the thirteen seelie courts. They avoided the royal keeps, to steer clear of the bulk of the forces, but they still killed and pillaged their way through the lands. They had to be stopped before they went any farther. Now that the seelie had finally dispatched their forces, it was time to intervene.

Havryll tilted his head. "Is that advisable? With Khal gone, my authority may be questioned."

"If anyone questions it, inform them I'll deal with them upon my return." He was itching to *deal* with someone. He might even draw a sword, rather than playing with their mind this time.

Havryll laughed. "All right. Have fun."

He intended to.

Rissa had never visited the Court of Bones. Southwest of the Autumn Court, one of the most central lands in Denarhelm, it was known for the strong coven of bone hags who sustained their magic with sacrifices. They killed anything, from little critters to great beasts, and used their essence to power their spells. In the old days, they'd even used the bones of folk, but that practice was now forbidden.

The Court of Bones was entirely matriarchal —for centuries, the women of the line of Roaryn had ruled it. Rissa had read about their history and knew the name of the current queen: Sura. She'd had seven daughters—no one bothered to record the boys—and every single one of them had been killed before they came of age. Rumor had it that Sura killed them herself, though Rissa had never believed it. At least, not before her chat with Teoran. Perhaps parents were capable of such deeds. She shouldn't assume everyone was like her father.

The fortress of Deanon didn't disappoint. Built in the shape of a skull made of red stone, carved beneath a solemn peak, it was positively monstrous.

"You seelie have interesting tastes in decor," Khal remarked casually as the ominous dwelling came in full view.

Teoran huffed, but there was little heat to his annoyance. He seemed otherwise concerned.

"What is it?"

"It's smoking."

Indeed it was, though Rissa had barely noticed. It stood to reason that a building designed to look like an immense skull exhaled smoke out of its nostrils and eye sockets. "Isn't it usually?"

Teoran shook his head. "Perhaps it would be wise to ride on. We could make for the Autumn Court."

She shook her head. "We're here now, and it'll be night before long."

While she preferred being active at night normally, she'd switched things around since the start of their journey; traveling during the day made more sense. During the night, on unfamiliar ground, they sought shelter, away from predators.

Khal sped up, riding ahead of their trio, although until now he'd seemed content to take up the rear. Rissa noticed the change in his expression. Silent and still, he seemed to watch everything, hear the slightest of feathers ruffling in trees, and turn to any sound, his sword hand set on his blade.

The warrior's alert made her wary. Their horses slowed to a trot as they neared the gates of the fortress.

"Who goes there!" a guard screamed from a post.

"Teoran Gaulder. I am known to your queen."

There was a pause, then the great iron gates opened with a slow, metallic squeal.

Khal was first to ride in, and his horse

stopped moments after passing through the gates. Rissa followed next, then Teoran.

Like Khal, she came to a sudden stop, gaping as she took in the sight before her.

The city was burning.

FLESH AND BONES

"**T**eo!" a fae screamed from a distance.

Tall and brown skinned, with luscious bone-gray hair, the fae looked like a young girl, but she moved with too much grace, and her deep, dark eyes told a very different tale.

This was an ancient. How ancient, Rissa couldn't guess.

"If you came here for the barbecue, you're too late, my friend." She laughed with good humor as she seized the reins of Teoran's steed, and led them through the narrow streets.

Barbecue? Half the houses were still on fire, and the other half had been scorched black. Charred corpses were piled up high on the paved ground. She seemed far too cheery for what they saw.

Rissa's eyes slid away from the fae and back to the corpses.

"What are these things?" she asked. They didn't smell like fae.

They didn't even look like fae, although Rissa hadn't had the displeasure of smelling burned folk before today. There was a strange, dark air of magic around them—magic she'd never felt or heard about before.

"Humans," said the stranger.

Rissa frowned, confused. Humans were creatures of nothing but flesh.

"Or something like it. They were too strong, and there was something strange in their eyes. As if their souls had left them. If I'm to guess, humans have been experimenting with dark magics again, in order to best us. It wasn't the first and won't be the last attempt." She shrugged.

Rissa would kill to have that confidence someday.

"You were attacked?" Khal asked.

The woman sneered. "I do not answer to your kind, southerner."

Teoran smirked, delighted to see Khal denigrated. "What happened?"

"My spies spotted them sniffing about, so I feigned a retreat. When they came to occupy Deanon, we set it on fire and sealed the gates. We burned their bitch asses for a while, and came back to kill whoever was left breathing." She delivered the entire speech with a grin.

Rissa laughed. "That was smart."

The woman shrugged. "Not everyone will agree. It'll take a while to rebuild, and plenty of money, too. Ruling bites." They'd reached the nose of the skull—the entry into the main palace, no doubt. "I'll house you for the night, and you'll have a roof and bread, but don't expect much else."

"A roof and bread are all we need. Thank you, Sura," Teoran said fondly.

So, this was the Bone Queen, Sura Kraver. Rissa should have guessed as much, but she couldn't picture this woman bearing seven daughters—or killing them, for that matter.

"I should introduce my company."

"Oh, please don't," Sura retorted with a snort. "Let us pretend I have no idea whose illustrious company I'm in. Respectfully, I have enough problems on my plate." Her smile never left as she spun to face Rissa. "We'll meet again officially, under other circumstances. We'll chat then. For now, I have fires to put out, houses to rebuild, and many mouths to feed."

Rissa didn't know what to say. This great queen had identified her somehow, and though she wasn't exactly falling at her feet, she was recognizing her authority. "I'll help, if I can," she offered. "I'm not terrible with water charms."

Sura hesitated for a short moment, before laughing. "Well, I can't see why not. Let's get your horses settled, and we can get back to work."

~

She hadn't misrepresented the extent of her abilities; Rissa's link to water was rather weak. Her natural affinity was earth, and air and fire came to her easily enough. Wielding water magic was the fruit of long years of study. It looked like the rest of the inhabitants of Deanon could relate. Though there were several gentry, few even bothered with magic, preferring to carry buckets full of water.

Rissa assisted by lifting the moisture up in the air and letting it rain down on the burning buildings, speeding the process up, house after house. By the tenth, her head was ready to explode—the focus level necessary to perform magic that wasn't instinctual to her was enough to make her head spin. She kept going until the last of the fire was extinguished.

For his part, Khal made his muscles his contribution, letting Queen Sura boss him around without a word of protest. He lifted great wooden beams to support the weaker buildings, moved stones, and dragged corpses till sweat beaded on his temples.

Teoran aided the builders shirtless, to the

delight of the onlookers. He certainly was pleasant enough to look at, his slender, tanned frame sculpted like the statue of a god.

Rissa was quite put out to find that he made no impression on her. She could objectively appreciate his beauty—the red hair, the piercing moss green eyes, and all that golden skin—but none of it set her core on fire the way the mere thought of a certain annoying king could.

Rydekar be damned. If he messed with her libido, she'd have to murder him out of spite.

"I think we've done what we can for the night!" Sura called. "Dinner will be served at the keep."

The crowd erupted in whistles and claps, only too glad to comply. Rissa followed the flow back to the entrance of Sura's palace. A banquet had been set around three lambs roasting on spits. An imp stirred a cauldron of thick herbal stew, while pixies flew around with trays of freshly baked bread. Rissa's stomach growled with need.

She stood in line to get to the meat, wondering if she might collapse before her turn came.

The cook in charge of turning the lambs handed Queen Sura a wicked footlong knife that could certainly serve as a sword in a pinch, and the queen cut the first piece as her court clapped eagerly. She served the generous piece of haunch in a ceramic bowl painted red at the edges. The stew was served over the meat.

Rissa licked her lips. Was she drooling?

The queen looked around the crowd, frowning. Then she spotted her, and waved her forward. Feeling awkward under the scrutiny, Rissa joined her at the center of the square.

To her astonishment, Sura handed her that first bowl.

"Well?" the Bone Queen prompted. "How does Your Highness like the fare of Deanon?"

Rissa stood helplessly for a beat too long, before lifting the bowl to her lips. She breathed the scent in before dipping her lip in the burning stew.

She closed her eyes, moaning. "It's delicious." She couldn't remember ever tasting anything quite as delightful. Rissa's appetite was directly linked to the amount of energy she used, and after hours of water work, she could have devoured an elephant. She dug in, enthused by the claps around her. She ate every single drop, using her hands to pick at the meat, and they watched until she was entirely done.

When she'd licked the last drop, Queen Sura whistled, and returned to the roast to serve herself, signaling the start of the feast. The rest of the crowd waited in line for their turn.

Hadn't Sura said she couldn't deal with announcing to her court Rissa was visiting? Yet she'd done just that, by delegating the honor of opening the banquet, for this was the duty of the person holding the highest rank. She might as well have had a page scream her name out loud.

Still uncomfortable, Rissa opted to stand apart, close to the entrance of the palace. She sat on the statue of a lion, using the feline's lean body as a back rest.

"That was foolish."

Rissa wrinkled her nose. "How do you move so silently?"

She hadn't heard or sensed Khal's approach, but he was leaning on the other side of the statue now.

"Practice. I shadow Rye all the time. Don't change the subject. You should never eat first—not unless you trust the one serving you."

She rolled her eyes. "I'm not Rye. No one wants to murder me."

Khal snorted. "You're Serissa Braer. The list of people who want nothing more than to murder you is probably long enough to fill an entire book."

"Well, poison isn't the way to do it." She wasn't entirely immune to the strongest ones, as her last night in the Old Keep had proven, but she couldn't be killed with it.

An imp child dashed by and waved at her, grinning wide enough to show her pointed fangs. Rissa waved back.

"Oh?" Khal wasn't done with his lecture. "So, say I slip you a few drops of elvenbane. How hard would it be to cut your head off while you're passed out?"

She hated that he was right. "Well, I'm not passed out."

Another fae approached and bowed low, before walking on his way. She inclined her head to acknowledge him.

"By chance. You shouldn't have taken a stranger's loyalty for granted."

Rissa found that she didn't like being told what to do by Khal any more than she did Rydekar. She lifted her chin. "She wouldn't have poisoned me in public, with that many witnesses."

Stranger after stranger passed before them. Rissa noticed how they made a point of reaching her corner, just to greet her. She still couldn't quite believe it, despite the repeated occurrence. This whole week didn't align with what had been her reality up until then.

"All those witnesses are loyal to her court, except for me, and maybe that buffoon." He waved toward Teoran, who was dancing a reel with two court ladies, played by an impromptu gathering of musicians.

Rissa smiled. He certainly knew how to enjoy himself. "Aren't you going to eat?" she asked Khal, if only to change the subject.

He shrugged, though he must also be starving.

Khal was never one to refuse food from what she'd observed on their short journey. Guessing the issue, she told him, "No one is going to mess with you for being unseelie."

He snorted. "Right."

Rissa sighed before hopping off her perch. "Come. Let's get you fed. I don't have any use for a withering knight."

The throng of folk parted to make way for her. "We can wait our turn," she stated.

The fae smiled, nodded, and let her pass in front of them till she'd reached the cook. "Your Grace. Can't get enough of my mechoui?"

"I could eat this every day," she admitted. "I'd love a little more, but only if there's enough to go around."

The cook puffed his chest. "Oh, there's plenty for everyone to have seconds." He cut another piece for her, then served Khal generously.

A thin puck armed with a ladle filled the shallow bowls with the stew.

Chin lifted, the man stared pointedly at Khal. "Well? What do you say, stranger?"

Put on the spot, Khal broke off a small piece of meat with his hands before stuffing it in his mouth. His eyes widened. "By the gods! What *is* this?"

The cook's baritone laugh reverberated in the

air. "You tell your southerner friends we cook the best meat here in the north, you hear? If they don't believe you, send them to me. I'll set them straight."

Rissa left them to discuss herbs and stuffing, lost in the finer art of cookery. Instead of returning to her lion, she roamed the square aimlessly, encountering bows and curtsies till she was snared into a sudden, unexpected jive.

Laughing and struggling to keep hold of her bowl, she let Teoran swing her through the square.

Again, an unwelcome reminder of Rydekar edged at the corner of her mind. He was the last person she'd danced with, after all.

Dancing with Teoran was nothing like dancing with Rydekar. She had fun, her heart light and filled with laughter. Rydekar's embrace was the opposite. Nerve-wracking. Too hot and too cold all at once. Disturbingly engaging her core.

"I'm getting dizzy." While that wasn't entirely true, dizziness was the least of her problems.

She was getting wistful, missing a man who certainly wasn't thinking about her right now.

"We've had a long day," Teoran said, slowing their dance to a stop. "I'll see that Sura has her people show us to our quarters."

She thanked him, letting him approach the

queen, who surveyed the square from the steps of her residence.

The queen was one to be hands on with the running of her court; she showed them the way herself, settling Rissa in a room more opulent than the one she'd occupied at her father's home. Although the gilded bone decor wasn't really to her taste.

Rissa practically leaped to the bed the moment she was left alone.

That was the first night she dreamt of him.

THE IN BETWEEN

She opened her eyes in the very same bed where Rydekar had left her three days past, but this time, he was lying down next to her, under the covers.

Quite conscious of the fact that she was in the City of Bones, she knew right away that she was dreaming.

Rydekar looked just as she remembered him, to the smallest crease of his eye, the slightest dip in his sensual lips.

"To what do I owe the pleasure?" His voice sounded groggy, as though he'd also been asleep.

"It's my dream. You tell me."

He laughed, the sound low and throaty. Then, shifting on the bed to close the distance between them, he hovered over her. Close enough for her to feel the heat of his breath. To catch his scent.

"Does this feel like a dream, Rissa dear?" His hand touched her forehead ever so softly, before brushing a curl off her forehead.

It didn't. Not at all. She could feel him, his hand, his heat.

"I'm not in the Old Keep. You're not with me." She couldn't make sense of it.

"Your body might be a little far, but it seems you've found your way to my bed all the same, princess." Rydekar chuckled. "The question is why."

She narrowed her eyes. "You're a smug bastard even in my imagination."

Rydekar chuckled, and the bed shook under him. "You don't have the creativity to imagine the likes of me. No, your mind reached out to me tonight." He smirked. "Did you miss me?"

She'd rather remove her fingernails with pincers than admitting as much. "How do I know *you* aren't the one invading my mind?"

"Because this is my room. If I came to you, we'd be wherever you're staying."

Damn him, but it made sense.

Rissa could only pout, and switch to another topic. "How does this work? I didn't know it was possible to reach someone's mind like this. It's... vivid. Is that a power of yours?"

He shook his head, seeming far too amused. "I'm not doing anything, princess."

"I thought I was a queen," she quipped.

He shrugged. "Act like it and we'll talk."

Bastard. Part of her wanted to tell him what had happened today. How the Court of Bones had seemed to embrace her without her doing anything. The crown she dreaded didn't seem quite so heavy up here, with these people.

Rydekar wouldn't care, though.

"Have you made it to the Wilderness yet?"

She shook her head. "We're in Deanon. It's been..." She hesitated. "Interesting."

"How so?" Rydekar asked, genuinely curious.

Rissa attempted to curb her excitement and seem casual. "They were nice to us. You know, welcoming. They were attacked, but burned the human soldiers." This, Rydekar would be interested in. "They were strange, Rye. There was an aura of magic around these corpses. Sura Kraver thinks they might have enhanced the human soldiers, using some sorcery. They burned all the same."

"The Bone Queen is known for her savagery. Good to hear her reputation wasn't exaggerated. Is Khal still with you? Are you safe?"

She was half surprised to hear him enquire after her, rather than asking about the soldiers, or Sura, or just about anything else. "I'm safe. Khal's in the room next to mine, and Teoran's not far either. I have no reason to think they wish us harm, so far."

Rydekar snorted. "You trust too readily."

She rolled her eyes. "Yeah, Khal thinks so too."

She proceeded to tell him about the banquet, and to her surprise, Rydekar listened, interrupting only to ask for clarification or laugh at something she said. He was the perfect conversationalist, here in her mind. Perhaps this was just a dream after all.

When she'd said everything she could think of about their travels, she enquired after him. Rydekar sighed. "I'm not in this room right now. I'm asleep, but in a very different bed."

She could feel her shoulders tense. "Whose?"

He laughed again, and his fingertip tapped her nose. "Jealousy suits you. Mine, Rissa. I'm in my tent, some miles north of Old Keep, resting before traveling on. We aren't far from your father's domain, in fact."

None of this was reassuring. "What happened?"

"War," he replied. "As you well know. I can't very well remain behind my walls and let the rest of the world spill their blood on my orders."

She remained silent. Somehow, she'd imagined just that: that he'd command his armies from the safety of Old Keep. The thought of him charging at enemies, risking his life, didn't sit well with her at all.

"What if you're killed?"

"Then there'll be songs sung in my honor, statues erected, and my name will pass into legends like my ancestors' before me, I suppose." He was so annoyingly casual about it.

Lips pursed, she sat up to face him, eyes narrowed. "You can't risk your life stupidly. Not in the middle of this. Who else could lead Tenebris? And Denarhelm for that matter. If you're gone, Antheos is going to take the entire fae world."

He stared at her with that maddening smile she couldn't quite read, half mocking, but also something darker—colder. "Yes, well. I suppose you'd better bring back a spare leader in case something happens to me."

She wanted to nod, but Teoran's rant about Tharsen not being the one they needed made her question everything. What if he was right? What if there were more than rumors to the cursed prince's cruelty?

"Tharsen is a military leader," she reasoned out loud. "During the rule of his mother, the seelie and unseelie realms were at war, and there was a constant threat from the west. He'll know what to do."

Then, after Antheos was dealt with, what would happen?

"You truly believe that, don't you?" Rydekar asked.

"Why don't you?" she questioned.

She needed to understand why he was so adamantly against her idea. From the very beginning, he hadn't hidden his contempt and disapproval, without giving her any reason why.

Then again, she hadn't asked.

"I've read enough to make a grown man tremble at the mention of Tharsen's name, but my great-great-grandfather was also feared by all those who heard of him—no less by those who knew him. Yet, he's a good man. There's a chance that your Tharsen might prove to be one too."

She perked up.

"A chance, Serissa, and not a great one. I like to deal with facts, and the fact is Denarhelm currently has a perfectly adequate ruler, and in all likelihood, changing it will not work to our advantage."

Rissa wondered why they'd never spoken like this before, openly sharing their thoughts rather than butting heads. She only took half the responsibility. Sure, she wasn't as amiable as she could be, but Rydekar usually did his best to get on her nerves, too.

"But there's also a chance that Tharsen will be great. Better than adequate, in any case. Right?" she offered.

Rydekar stared on before sighing. "It's possible. I'd still prefer to stick to the odds we had with you here."

Something moved inside her; her heart, perhaps. He believed in her. He thought she was capable of things she wouldn't ever have thought herself capable of. Ruling an entire mighty fairy kingdom.

"How about this? I'll come back with Tharsen. That way, you'll get him—someone the seelie lords can follow—and me. I'll do what I can to help. This is my world too."

Rydekar laughed uproariously, throwing his head back.

She glared. She might not always read him easily, but she could tell when he was mocking her.

"It's sweet you think you have a choice in the matter. Khal will bring you back to the Old Keep."

He said so with absolute certainty.

"What if I don't want him to?"

She wished she could wipe Rydekar's smirk off his smug face. "You will."

She awoke full of energy, after a sleep that had proved deep and restful. Rissa didn't dream after Rydekar faded away from her mind. Part of her wondered if their interaction had been the product of her imagination, but to her annoyance, he'd been right: she wouldn't have been able to picture him quite so clearly of her own accord.

Rissa found the clothing she'd removed before bed laundered. She put them back on, grateful; her leather ensemble certainly had seen better days after three days of travel.

She'd only just dressed when a knock resounded at the door. "Come in!"

Khal entered, clothed, with his cloak and bags at hand. She frowned. "Are we in a rush?"

"If you want to make the Wilderness before dark, yes. We can reach the borders today."

She nodded, slowly, suddenly less sure. She liked the idea of remaining here for a few hours. Maybe for a day. She also liked the thought of returning to the Keep, but if she did without even attempting her initial goal, what would Rye say? She didn't like the thought of being so easily swayed. She ought to try, at least.

"All right. I'd like to see the queen, first."

"Sura. Call her Sura. You're the only queen who matters here."

Rissa sighed. When had she stopped protesting that title? So many things had changed in the span of just a few days, her reality seemed to fade away beneath her feet.

"Right. Do you know where she is?"

He shook his head. "I'll find out. Can you gather your things?"

He was in a rush to get going.

Rissa hadn't bothered to unpack before collapsing the previous day. Checking her inventory, she noticed that the rest of her clothing had also been laundered. Nothing was missing from her bag at first glance. Whoever had taken care of the room was honorable—and silent.

Teoran knocked shortly after Khal left. Unlike the rest of them, he seemed far from ready. In fact, he seemed like he was just now coming back after spending the entire night drinking and dancing. Khal wasn't going to like this one bit.

"I see you had fun."

He groaned, wincing to better deal with the brightness filtering through the windows. "Don't you start. Khal's lecture was all I can take. I'm ready to go, if we must though."

He truly wasn't. "Teoran, you should stay here." He didn't like the idea of waking Tharsen up any more than Rydekar. Or Khal.

Why was she the only one who saw the merit of her plan?

That certainly woke him up. "*What?*"

She shrugged. "The Wilderness is dangerous. Khal volunteered for this—you didn't know where we were going. And you don't want to wake Tharsen anyway."

"Why would what I want matter?" he questioned, truly confused.

"It should matter."

The prince shook his head. "I know you're new to this, but let me explain the situation as best I can. You're the queen. I'm a lowly prince of a small court. You've accepted my company, therefore, I will live, fight, and die to protect you until such a time as you dismiss me, as the laws of honor dictate." His voice was clipped, and rising in anger. "Are you dismissing me?"

She blinked, taken aback. Was she?

Something told her that this wasn't to be taken lightly. Dismissing him would affect them both for much time to come. How, she didn't want to know. "No."

"Well, then. To the Wilderness."

Khal located Queen Sura in a music room, two floors above the living quarters. He came to escort them back, and catching the tension between Teoran and Rissa, he did so in an uncomfortable silence.

The queen was seated among a flock of lords and ladies, listening to a lone singer's tender, lamenting story of heartbreak that ended in disaster.

When Rissa entered, Sura got to her feet, gesturing the company to continue their entertainment.

They walked together to a small chamber adjacent to the music room, a library filled with books on every wall, from floor to ceiling.

"I'd like to thank you for your hospitality,

Sura," she said, choosing to follow Khal's advice as to how to address the illustrious personage.

The queen wasn't fooled. "And you'd like to order me about, too," she guessed, one eyebrow crooked.

Rissa bit her lip.

"Go on. Give it a go," Sura said encouragingly. "I'm sure you'll do fine."

"I believe it's in all our interest for you and your court to head south. You can take care of yourself, that much is clear. But if the entire kingdom falls, and you're surrounded by enemies on all fronts, you'll be destroyed all the same. I don't want you to be the last to fall. I'd have you come back and thrive, after we put this invasion behind us."

Sura perused every inch of Rissa, before breaking into a smile. "Now, that wasn't that bad, was it?"

Rissa winced. "I didn't like it."

"Good." Sura nodded. "A high queen shouldn't be too fond of power. If you keep the leash too tight, the dogs may just turn around and bite. I'll go south as you demand, but let us be clear. I will not answer to that unseelie boy, regardless of whether you two are sharing a bed."

Rissa's cheek flamed. Rumors had traveled at the speed of light. "I don't expect you to obey Rydekar in all things, but I will have you support him in his endeavor to keep our kingdoms safe. Can you do that?"

The Bone Queen chuckled. "So long as everything he says agrees with my way of seeing things, I don't see why not."

Rissa smirked. "Sounds good to me."

Rydekar was going to *hate* her.

SINUOUS

A sea of twisted trees expanded as far as the eyes could see, through waves of hills and mountains. From the height of Peak Treas, at the edge of the Autumn Court territory and the Wilderness, they could survey almost all of the land.

"It's beautiful." She'd never seen a forest so abundant and richly filled with life. It resonated deep inside her.

"And insanely dangerous," Teoran quipped.

Rissa knew better than to offer for him to stay behind again. He'd truly been offended the previous day.

After a long ride, with only two breaks for the sake of the horses, they'd reached the edge of the Wilderness last night and elected to stay in a hunting lodge that belonged to Teoran's family. Unused in winter, it had been cold and empty, but it had a roof and enough wood to build fires. First thing in the morning, they'd journeyed farther north. This was their first view of the Wilderness. Rissa didn't need to ask why it was called that now. The dense conglomeration of trees, and endless plains were undisturbed by any building. Men and folk alike had left this land intact.

Rissa realized this was all appearances. The Wilderness was home to some of the most powerful of the folk; they simply preferred to remain closer to nature. The courtless—shy folk, wild folk, and the fire-breathers of Anondarth called these lands their own.

"Ready?"

Was she?

This place was home to someone else. Her mother. The woman who'd brought her to her father's doorstep and left her without turning back.

Nightmares weren't known as the mothering sort. She didn't take it personally, but what if they met here? Would she recognize her? Would she care?

Rissa chastised herself for even sparing it a thought. "As I'll ever be."

There also was a chance her father might be here. After all, he'd come to the Wilderness on his last retreat, which was how she'd come to be.

The fruit of his dalliance with an inhabitant of these woods.

"We can turn back if you wish."

Rissa shook her head. They'd made it so far.

The path down Treas was long and perilous for the horses. They took their time to ensure none of them slipped. "Perhaps we should have left the horses behind," Rissa said.

Khal grunted his assent. "We might have to do so. There's no road. I doubt they'll pass easily in the thick of the forest."

The start of the trek down the other side of the hill proved him right when they had to dismount and lead their horses through sinuous paths barely ever walked. Still, none of them relished the thought of abandoning their mounts. There was no guarantee that they'd find them again on the way home, and what then? They may have taken just about four days to reach the Wilderness, but without horses, their return would take weeks. There was no guarantee they could find a ride anywhere, given that most of the courts ought to be traveling south by now.

Strenuous as their slow trudge could be, Rissa relished it. The smells were different here, purer and stronger. She identified a thousand things, and her nose picked up on so many more that she was hard-pressed to name.

She wasn't under the misconception that they

were alone. There had been eyes on them every-where in the last five days: eyes of birds, little folks, prey and predators alike. South of the Wilderness, the things that looked at them had wisely chosen to give them a wide berth. Few creatures were more dangerous than high fae, well-armed and in good shape. Here, the sense of safety Rissa felt—based on what she was—left her. There were things in the shadow of the forest, things that didn't fear them.

"I wonder what'll attack first. Some insane rogue, a pack of shades? Wait, I know! Dragons." Teoran was poorly hiding a healthy dose of fear beneath the sarcasm.

Khal managed a snarl that sounded like a laugh at the same time. "If you're afraid, you're very welcome to run back home, little princeling."

"Was that supposed to be an insult? Rich, coming from a fellow princeling."

"I was leading armies before you were born, boy. We aren't on the same playground."

"Oh, for the sake of everything holy, would you both stop?" If she was forced to deal with their testosterone for another day, she was going to explode. "You should just fuck and get it over with."

Khal glanced at Teoran, taking him in from head to toe, as if seriously considering Rissa's suggestion. He blew a breath. "I doubt he could take it."

"Bend over and find out," Teoran shot back.

Marvelous. Instead of pissing on each other's boots, they were now engaging in a flirting battle. Rissa made a mental note to offer to take the first watch when they stopped to rest tonight. If what it took for them to play nice was some hate-fucking, she was more than happy to help move things along.

They reached a clearing bathed in sunlight, where dainty flowers were growing in the thick of the winter. "We could stop here for a while," Rissa proposed.

It was almost time to eat. She'd gotten into the habit of taking a few bites every four hours or so, to keep her energy up throughout the day. Who knew when they'd find another convenient stop again?

Khal shook his head slowly, eyes on the forest floor. Following the direction of his gaze, Rissa noticed a bed of mushrooms growing close to their feet. They were white, with bright red teardrops running along their skin like rubies. They formed an almost perfect spiral, too purposeful to be natural. Or harmless.

"Is that—"

"A fairy ring," Khal said.

Designed to trick witless mortals into binding themselves to the world of the fae, they'd long been outlawed, though Rissa had seen drawings in her school books. "Aren't they supposed to be circular?"

"Certainly. If they're meant for humans," Khal replied.

They carefully threaded around the mushrooms, and returned to the path. Were they even going the right way? From up on the hill, spotting the general direction they should take had been easy enough, but down here, the thick cover of tree branches made her lose all notion of location.

Rissa rummaged through her pack till she found what she was looking for, extricating her old compass. She also had a map of Denarhelm somewhere, but Teoran's presence had rendered it redundant.

The map was useless now; no one had ever mapped the Wilderness. The compass was equally inutile. Its needle, supposed to point north, turned round and round at full speed. Magic could mess with the planet's magnetic signature, and in this place, it was everywhere, clogging the air with too much energy.

She glanced up. "I should climb, to check we're going east."

"We're going east," Teoran assured.

"It wouldn't hurt to be certain," Khal said. "I can make the climb."

"I *am* certain." Teoran glowered.

"How? Have you been here before?" she asked, surprised he hadn't mentioned it until now.

"Because the sun rises in the east and sets in

the west. It's just before midday, it's still eastward, and I can feel it, prick." His expression lightened when he glanced at Rissa. "Being sensitive to the change in light is particular to the four seasonal courts. You should be able to feel it too, right?"

Rissa was noncommittal. "Hm."

She never liked to admit that she hadn't taken much power from her father at all. She had her link to the land, and the skillset of a nightmare. She'd learned to harness and control all elements, as most gentry could. But the specific powers of Titus or Mab had always lurked beyond her reach. She had no idea where the sun actually was beyond the cover of branches.

"I say we climb anyway. Not to doubt the princeling," Khal snorted, his tone very much doubting him, "but we might see a better path for the horses."

Teoran gruffly nodded.

Rissa hopped on the trunk, grateful to take a breather from these two. The tree was thick, strong, and so filled with life, it seemed to have a mind of its own. Perching on a low-hanging branch, she removed one of her leather gloves, pressing her palm against its bark. Then she felt it. Its will, its history. As if aware that she was trying, willing, or simply able to communicate with it, the tree drowned her mind under a flow of images. Its history, from acorn to sapling. She saw bare feet walk on the forest ground. Songs sung by the teardrops feeding its life force. And something else. A sense of belonging to this forest, to these lands, to this world. This tree was fae. It was folk. Maybe it had sap and branches rather than blood, but it very much considered itself a wild thing. And it was.

Rissa caressed the branch in a soothing motion. She couldn't tell where the melody that crossed her lips came from, but she hummed it all the same.

"Whoa!" She grabbed the branch with both hands, struggling to stay upright, as the branch extended below her feet, taking her up, higher and higher. When it reached as far as it could go, another branch curved to reach her. She leapt on it, and settled down as it lifted her. Rissa grinned. She'd never minded climbing herself, but this was a lot more fun.

The tree carried her to the very top, above the line of leaves blocking the view. She blinked, the strength of the sunlight blinding her eyes. They'd been used to darkness for the last few hours.

From up there, she could see they were close to the center of the forest, and indeed, they had been marching east.

A solitary mount dominated the horizon, higher than any hills or peaks. Even miles away, she could see the sheer wall of spells shielding it.

The forbidden mountain. They were almost

there, close enough to reach it by the end of the night if they continued at this pace.

Excitement clogging her chest, she started to climb down, eager to inform her companions of their progress.

She was only halfway to the ground when the previously friendly branch hit her flank hard enough to bruise. Before she could recover, it plastered her against the tree trunk and curved around it twice, capturing her in place.

She opened her mouth to scream. A vine wrapped around her mouth, nose, and eyes, engulfing her in a deadly embrace.

NEW FRIENDSHIPS

A rising sense of panic sent her heartbeat into a gallop. Rissa forced herself to focus, reluctantly ready to lash out. She hated the thought of harming a tree, but she also had no intention of letting it bury her beneath its trunk.

Suddenly, the vines around her eyes parted, along with some of the branches under her feet, giving her a clear view of the forest floor.

Teoran and Khal were on their knees, facing the tree trunk, hands above their heads. Five warriors dressed in nothing but low-hanging skirts held them at lance-point, discussing among themselves and pointing to the tree. They knew she was up there; they were arguing about how to get to her.

Had the tree truly meant to help her? She knew it had a consciousness of sorts, but she wouldn't have expected it to be so reactive, so aware of the world around it.

"You're a good tree, aren't you?" The branches moved ever so slightly, their flutter caressing her skin. It liked the praise. "I'm going to need you to free me." Harming it was out of the question now that she realized it was just trying to keep her safe, but she needed out of there all the same. "I have to help my friends."

The branches around her tightened, squeezing her too tight. Dammit.

She let a frustrated breath out.

"Let's talk about this reasonably. As a tree, I'm guessing you have a set of needs." The branches were still, enrapt. She'd been right. Like anything with a soul, the tree was bribable. The question was, what could she promise a damn tree? Rain? Squirrel nests?

Unexpectedly inspired, Rissa grinned. "You know, I live rather far from here, and there aren't many trees as strong and tall as you. I could carry your acorns south, sow a few of them in our fields. Your legacy could reach the entire fae kingdom."

Oh, she had its attention now.

"Just help me with my friends."

The tree remained motionless for several moments, before the branches untangled around her torso. "That's it. Good tree. Now, I'll get down there and..."

The tree didn't agree. Branches shot toward the ground, fast as thunder, plunging into the ground right under the kneeling fae's backs, separating them from their captors. The five warriors barely had the time to step back, before roots erupted, lashing out like whips.

"Or that. That's good, too." Her branch lowered her to Khal and Teoran's level. She rushed to undo the fine rope binding their wrists.

"All right, what the hell is that?" Teoran's voice was three octaves above his usual tone, and he stared at the tree like it was going to eat him alive.

Which, to be fair, it might.

"Another time?" Rissa suggested. "We'd better scamper."

They might have taken them by surprise, but if these five warriors had managed to incapacitate both Teoran and Khal, she wanted to get as far away from them as possible.

"The horses!" Teoran hissed. They were on the other side of the barrier of branches.

"We have to go," she repeated.

Their choices were attacking or fleeing, and she didn't like the idea of making the local folk their enemies before they'd even reached their destination.

Khal was with her on this; he nodded before leading the way, setting off at a jog.

Rissa bent down and picked up a handful of acorns to stuff in her pocket before joining them.

They left the screams of their attackers behind—the tree must have kept on thrashing at them. But for how long? Those people would be on their trail, eventually. Without the horses, they had little chance of outrunning them on their own territory.

Were they even still going the right way?

They reached a rift, so sharp the trench underneath seemed hundreds of miles down.

Crap. What now?

"There's a bridge down here," Khal said, pointing to his left.

Rissa turned to Teoran. He was panting, bent over, hands on his knees. Endurance mustn't be his strongest trait. "Wouldn't that take us too far from where we're supposed to go? That's leading west, right?"

He looked up. Sweat was pouring down his hairline, making his skin shimmer. Rissa grabbed the bota bag she kept in her red satchel and handed it to him. They were going to have to ration water and food. Most of their supplies had been with the horses.

Teoran wasn't on the same wavelength; he drank like he was moments away from dying of thirst.

"What happened?" she asked, glancing back.

"I wasn't up there for long, but when I came back down—"

"They were waiting for you to go," Khal guessed. "They attacked us right after you disappeared up into the tree. How did you do that? Make the tree move."

Teoran handed her what was left of her water; she gave it to Khal, who took one sip before handing it back.

"I didn't make it do anything. It wanted to. I think it liked the company. People mustn't pay attention to it often, and it has a consciousness. It craved a connection."

Teoran snorted. "Rissa. It's a tree."

She shrugged. "Well, that tree saved your skin."

Rissa glanced back at the line of trees they'd just left, and turned to the rift, an insane thought flirting at the edge of her mind. She bit her lip. It probably was impossible. But what would it cost to try?

"We have to move," Khal said.

He wasn't wrong, but first, she wanted to give her idea a try.

"Two seconds." Rissa ran back to the closest tree, and placed her gloveless hand on its trunk.

At first, there was nothing at all. She almost removed it. Then she felt a small tinge of awareness burn under her skin. This one was also alive. Younger, it had far less character than Rissa's latest friend, and she could feel a surly, carefree outlook. She glanced up. This tree was barely two meters tall—a baby.

This wasn't going to be easy.

"Want to help out?"

She felt nothing, no movement, no response.

"Want to piss off those who live in the forest?" Now there was a tinge, the slightest flicker. "I bet they cut down plenty of trees for heat. I bet you've seen friends knocked down. I bet you're *angry*."

Oh yes, it was.

"They want to catch us. If you helped get us across, they won't be able to. And in return, I could bring an acorn to the other side. How about that?" The technique had worked once, but this specific tree didn't care for its acorns. It was deliberating, unsure she was worth the bother.

"What do you want, then?" Rissa couldn't quite believe she was wasting her time negotiating with a tree.

If it was able to communicate, it didn't bother.

They couldn't remain here indefinitely. "I could make you taller. Taller than your friends here. Stronger, too."

The branches fluttered with unconcealed excitement. She got it.

The ground under their feet shook. Khal adopted a fighting stance, legs spread apart, hand on the hilt of his sword, facing the forest. Even Rissa half expected to see an army of enemies rush out, but what came out of the shadows of the woods were rows after rows of ground-creeping plants, slithering like snakes, or lashing out. She stumbled backward, keeping out of their way.

The ivy crawled to the rift, twisting, curving, and extending until it knotted itself in the shape of a bridge, just large enough for one person to come across at the time.

"How are you doing any of that?"

A fair question that didn't truly have an answer. "I'm not. The forest is."

Never one to go back on a bargain, she released some of her energy through the young oak tree, letting its roots dig deeper and its trunk extend higher. Then she dashed out to the newly formed bridge.

Khal tested the strength of the hedera ivy, dubious as ever. "I'll go first. If it breaks, we'll never survive the fall."

"I'm lighter," Rissa pointed out.

Both men growled low in their throats.

"You're *not* trying an unstable knot of branches flying over a thousand-mile drop." Teoran huffed. "Besides, I could be lighter than you. *I'll* go."

She didn't like the thought—this was her idea, she ought to be the one experimenting. Not to mention, if she fell, there was a chance the ivy might try to do something about it. Teoran was already gone, his assured footfalls light and swift over the evergreen twists.

Once he reached the other side, he held one hand up, yelling, "It's stable enough!"

Khal gestured Rissa forward.

It hadn't escaped her that she was always in the middle. Khal either took the front or rear, ensuring she was guarded on both sides. Part of her protested against the ever-vigilant attention, but she was growing used to it. The man was so used to living in his cousin's shadow, he probably didn't know how to put himself first.

Her first step was far from what she would have qualified as stable; the ivy had tried its best, but the surface was still uneven. Beyond the tips of her leather boots, she could spot the depth of plunge. Swallowing a thick lump down, she lifted her gaze to Teoran, and walked slowly and carefully. She couldn't resist another look down.

Her stomach dropped to her feet.

"Come on!" Teoran waved from the other side. "Don't think about it. You'll make it."

She nodded. Right. If he'd managed with ease, there was no reason why she couldn't make it to the other side. She was already halfway.

Another step, then a third.

A racket called her attention back to the forest, moments before an arrow flew right past her, landing on the ivy.

She swore out loud, ducking to avoid it.

"Run!" Khal roared, pulling his sword.

Shapes darkened the shadows of the forest, approaching fast, and the idiot was planning to fight them.

"You run!" she yelled back.

Staying low, she crawled along the ivy, closing her eyes to avoid looking down, or back at the forest. "You'd better be on this bridge, Khalven!"

Reaching the other side, she hopped to her feet and turned to look back.

Khal had waited for her to get to safety, the fool, but he was getting on the bridge now, just as the half-naked warriors came into view, one armed with an arrow, the others holding their lances at eye level. Another problem came to her attention: the ivy was untangling, retreating from their side of the bridge.

"Khal!" she urged.

He lowered his sword and focused on darting to them, as the bridge withdrew right beneath his feet.

No, no, no. Fear gripped her spine, icy, shortening her breath. He couldn't die. He couldn't be hurt. Rydekar would never forgive her if his cousin was harmed during the quest he already saw as pointless. Khal was charming, caring, and he didn't deserve this. He had to make it.

Teoran threw his knife with precision, almost

hitting the archer. The next arrow flew toward them. He was attempting to get the attention of the warrior on them, rather than Khal, Rissa guessed. He only half succeeded; lances were still flying right past Khal, hitting the disentangling bridge.

He reached the end of the ivy path and prepared to jump across. He could make it—it was two yards.

Khal was in midair, and she opened her hand over the rift, ready to catch him if he ended up jumping a few feet short, when a sharp cry filled the air. Hers, his, she couldn't tell.

The tip of a lance pierced his shin, breaking his stride.

The last thing she saw was the expression on his face. Confusion. Fear.

Then he fell.

BEYOND THE WALL

Fear. Horror. Something else underneath. Something cold.

Rydekar dismissed the feelings that assaulted his mind, recognizing them for what they were: hers.

Strange that he could sense her so clearly when they'd never done anything to bond, but that was one problem he would concentrate on later.

He stood at the front, facing four seelie warriors, all of whom seemed to relish the thought of planting their blades in his back. They may be on the same side today, but he had to keep his wits about him in such company.

"So, you're the boy," said the Bone Queen.

Her size, youth and beauty were weapons she wielded expertly. So were her words.

He lifted his chin. "So, you're the murderous

bitch who kills her children before they come of age," he retorted smoothly.

They had to learn to share the battlefield, but if she wasn't playing nice, there was no reason why he should.

Queen Sura huffed a laugh. "At least you have some balls on you. And you're pretty enough to look at, I suppose. I told my queen I'd come to help. Here I am, but I'll do things my way. If you try to order me, I'll eat out of your skull. Understood?"

"You've seen Titus's child?" the other fae lord asked.

As tall as Sura was short, the king of the Iron Court, Siobhe's father, boasted long silver hair and metallic eyes with barely any white. The members of Iron Court purposely poisoned themselves with silver to access darker magic— and to ensure their very blood could be used as a weapon against other folk. As their ruler, Folker drank twice as much as anyone else.

"Aye, the high queen came to us," Sura said, grinning victoriously.

There didn't seem to be any love lost between these two.

"Where is she, then?" Folker snarled. "I wish to discourse with her directly. It's unheard of— moving the armies out of their respective courts, letting the unseelie come through our borders..."

"She's where she needs to be," said a child-like voice, sweet as morning dew.

The ruler of the White Court was an actual little girl; she must be Nyla's age, if that. Pale as starlight, with a white blindfold over her eyes, the only color on her was her ink-black lips.

The White Army was the creepiest thing Rydekar had ever had the displeasure to behold. Every single soldier, every commander, every advisor was a child, not even out of puberty. And all of them were blindfolded.

He supposed that magic was keeping them in this form; they may not be actual children. Right? Why, he didn't want to ask. All he wanted was to get this over with, so they could return to their home and never be seen again.

Sura nodded, agreeing with the child. She didn't seem to mind the fact that the fellow queen looked like a six-year-old. "You and I can worry about unseelie forces after we deal with the human scum."

Glaring at Rydekar, Folker acquiesced.

Rydekar didn't care one bit about what they thought of him. He wanted their armies to fight against Antheos, nothing more, nothing less.

"My men and I will hold anything south of the city." They were close to Orach, in the Court of Stars. "I just need you to stay north and alert us if you see any movement. What they've taken of Denarhelm so far, we can rebuild later. Let's ensure they don't encroach into fae land any farther."

He turned his back on them, not bothering to wait for an answer.

"That went well," Crane noted, without any irony.

"Well, there was no murder."

As he returned to his tent, his mind tuned back into the phantom feeling he'd rejected earlier, instinctively checking on Rissa.

She must be in the Wilderness by now, and her fear didn't bode well. She wasn't harmed; he would have *known* it if she was.

Nothing. No fear, no panic. He'd lost the thread leading him to her. Frustrated, he abandoned his endeavor as Morgan approached.

"Well?" He sounded shorter than he meant to be.

"They've stopped progressing south. My theory is, their own spies saw we organized a line of defense. From what I can see, they're hunting down whatever fae they can find in the lands they've already taken." His spymaster wrinkled her nose in distaste. "You don't want to know what they do to those they catch. These people aren't normal humans. They're barbarians."

"We'll push through a mile north in the morning." Rydekar turned to Denos. "Inform the commanders I want them in the tent."

He returned to his tent and bent over the

map that used to be set in his war room. Again, his eyes hovered over the Wilderness for one moment, before returning to Denarhelm.

He couldn't afford any distractions right now, and that was exactly what thoughts of Rissa were. Distractions that could get his men killed.

She was fine for now, and that was all he needed to know.

~

She fell on her knees. Sounds and vision disappeared; there was nothing but a drowning gulf of emptiness around her.

He'd fallen. He was dead. Because of her. Because she'd insisted on coming here, and she'd had her grand ideas with her trees. She'd made decisions and her companion, her friend, was dead because of her.

"Get up. We need to go. Rissa!" Teoran cursed, grunting. "Rissa!"

The last scream got through to her. Suddenly, in front of her eyes, there were five monsters, throwing blades and arrows at them. The monsters who'd killed Khal.

Fury coursed through her veins. She wanted blood. She'd extricate it slowly, painfully.

"Rissa!" Teoran pulled her sleeve, trying to get her up.

She got to her feet, trembling with rage.

"They'll find a way to our side. Come on."

But she was done running.

Rissa screamed. She yelled at the top of her lungs, reaching out to a part of her she seldom even acknowledged, let alone used. Now, she gave into it, coaxing it out, letting it spread its venom.

The sky darkened, clouds gathering overhead, blocking the sunlight. She wasn't ordering that. If it was the price for her magic, she was more than willing to pay it.

Behind the warriors, the forest trembled, as if by a stampede. Vines, roots, and branches shot out straight. The five men started to run. She grinned at them, showing teeth. Oh, it was far too late for that. She watched as their bones were crushed and twisted, savoring each scream, each crack.

Then there was nothing but silence. Roots and branches and vines curved back where they belonged. She was left with nothing. Emptiness. Guilt.

She liked Khal. He was fun, loyal, protective, and funny, although his sense of humor had mostly been focused on aggravating Teoran. And now he was gone. Nothing, no amount of blood could fill that void.

"He was a good man," Teoran said.

"You hated him," Rissa retorted, spitting the accusation. "You hated him because he was unseelie. How stupid is that? Rydekar was right. We're weak and blind and stupid because we're divided by nonsense. He was good, and you hated him for no reason!" She wanted to yell, but she couldn't manage more than a whisper.

Too shocked to move, too guilty to let herself feel anything else—even sorrow—she remained on her knees and let herself cry.

Teoran placed a hand on her shoulder, attempting no other words. Good thing too; she would have jumped at his throat given half a chance. Anger was easier than this. Anything was easier than the loss of something that she didn't quite understand. Khal felt like he'd been part of her; part of a life she'd never get the chance to live now.

"I didn't hate him. I envied him."

Rissa would have called bullshit if she had the strength.

"Like me, he's a youngest son, yet he was valued by everyone. Wherever he went, people respected him at first glance. He was a candle in the dark—someone we naturally gravitate to. Khal was beautiful in and—"

"Don't be shy. Keep going. Maybe throw me a rope first, though?"

Shock jolted her upright, and she advanced so fast she almost fell through the gap.

A single root twisted around his middle, Khal

was climbing up the smooth surface of the rift as best he could.

"You arse! Didn't it occur to you to, oh, I don't know, let us know you were alive!" Teoran screeched.

Rissa seconded the sentiment, but she was too busy laughing to formulate any word.

"I tried. You guys seemed too busy screaming and everything."

"Come up here. I'm going to strangle you. You hear? Strangle you!"

Rissa called to the branches again. She'd never done so before in her life, but it came naturally to her now. They stretched out from their side of the rift, curling around Khal to lift him up to their level.

"Just so you know, this is creepy," he said when he reached them.

Rissa jumped into his arms, shoving her wet face against his chest.

"Oh, all right. We're hugging now." He grimaced. "Can you try not to mention that to Rydekar?"

"How did you hang on?" Teoran questioned.

"I didn't," he admitted, pointing to the branch still twisting around him. "This just caught me. It's stronger than it looks."

The branch wasn't hanging on to anything at all. Inspecting it, Rissa would have sworn it was familiar. Too thin for a bigger tree, it seemed to belong to a briar of sorts, maybe roses.

As she watched it, the vine-like branch untwisted itself, and crawled along Khal's torso, reaching Rissa, although she stepped back. It glided along her hand, then snaked inside her skin, inserting itself painlessly in her veins like it belonged there.

Which it did.

The thing was one of her branches, the ones that had slithered along her skin since the day she was born. They'd never left her before.

She kept watching her empty hand, stunned.

"Well, thank you for that, I guess."

"I didn't do anything." She shook her head. "Except put you in danger. Those people were hunting us, and who knows how many will come after us next? We should never have come here."

The two men were silent, but she knew they agreed.

"What now?"

They had two choices, head back, or continue.

"Let's vote," Rissa offered. It was their lives, too; she wasn't going to dictate it. "All in favor of turning back?"

Only one hand was raised.

Hers.

THE CURSE

R ain poured incessantly, drenching every layer of clothing. Huffing, Rissa ended up bundling her cloak and throwing it in her bag. It wasn't doing any good, but if she managed to dry it, she might be able to use it as a cover when they finally found a place to rest.

They'd walked all day and barely made any progress. The forest seemed unending. She climbed a few times to check their location. There was little chance of reaching the mountain today, now that they'd lost the horses.

"We should pick a place to rest," she said when her feet started to complain.

"In the mud?" Teoran scowled. "No thanks."

Khal, never one to miss an opportunity to diss him, jeered, "The princeling is too delicate for a bit of mud."

Teoran grunted, but didn't attempt to defend himself. He hadn't said a word against Khal since the rift.

"We can take to the trees," Rissa suggested.

"I don't do well with heights." Khal grimaced. "It might be our best shot here, though."

Glad to have a semblance of consensus, Rissa hopped on the closest consequential tree and started her work, twisting nearby branches into hammocks. She managed to direct some of the larger leaves to cover them from the worst of the rain.

Climbing up, Teoran whistled.

"I've slept in worse places," Khal admitted. "I'll take the first watch."

"No," she replied, adamant. "I'll take it."

There was little chance of her sleeping anytime soon. The last day had been too emotionally draining, and her flight-or-fight response was still engaged. Besides, she wasn't the one who'd almost died. Though he hid it well, Khal had to be exhausted. Either way, he'd earned the rest.

"You're sure?" Teoran frowned. "I can take it."

She shook her head, managing a half smile. "You guys rest."

They settled in their makeshift beds, and she hopped down to the ground to start her watch.

Rissa leaned back against the tree, under the hammocks, trying to dry off a little. The moisture in the air didn't help. Her mind still reeling, she opted to patrol around their camp, listening carefully and watching the long shadows.

The warriors had been on them too fast, too silently. They could be watched even now.

Remembering that they'd waited for her to be out of the way before attacking, Rissa decided to venture a little farther, though she kept her senses fixed on their tree.

Finding a river, she filled her wineskin, pretending to be entirely engrossed with her task.

She wouldn't have caught the change in the shadows if she hadn't been watching for it. Moving fast as an arrow, she reached the place where she'd detected the movement and brought her knife to the enemy's neck.

"Got you."

"I suppose you have."

That voice.

Rissa knew that voice. Amused, detached, soft, cruel, and so very beautiful. It called to her like her own name. "And what are you going to do with me now?"

She tightened her grip on the knife. "Who are you?"

But she knew who the stranger was. She just wanted her to say it.

The thing chuckled and brushed her hand aside, spinning gracefully to face her.

The thing had her dark curls, her mouth, her straight nose, skin of a dark blue marked with silver vines, and dark eyes sprinkled with stars.

"You know who I am, daughter." Her mother, the stranger she hadn't seen since the day she'd been left at Titus's doorstep with a note and a name, grinned, showing sharp fangs. "Your nightmare."

She tightened her grip on the blade. "Did you send the assassins?"

Her mother tilted her head. "Why would I?"

That wasn't an answer, but Rissa didn't care to push for one. "What are you doing here?"

"What can I say?" She shrugged. "Curiosity. There aren't many nightmares in these lands, and I know their taste. You smelled different. I thought it might be you."

"Why would you care?"

"I don't," her mother replied smoothly, not bothering to lie.

Rissa held on to the knife with a death grip, fighting against the desire to release it.

"Well, your curiosity is satisfied, I'm sure. You can go."

Her mother smiled. "I certainly could. I would like to extend you my hospitality this night, however."

Rissa cackled. Hospitality. Her mother wanted to play nice now, after over a hundred years. "You must be joking."

The nightmare shrugged. "It's raining hard. You might enjoy some comfort until the sky is appeased."

"You sent assassins after us."

Her mother sighed. "I sent nothing. This isn't the courts. Assassins do as they please in these lands. You'll be safe in the haven. And dry."

Dry sounded good, drenched as she was, but the thought of accepting anything from this woman made bile rise in her throat.

Rissa's eyes returned to the hammocks. At the end of the day, her preference mattered little. Khal might have died today because of her, and he deserved a night out of this torrent, at the very least.

"Do I have your word I and my companions will be safe through the night?" she worded her request carefully.

"You do, daughter."

"Don't call me that." She didn't want this woman to call her anything. "My name is Serissa. You should remember. You picked it."

The nightmare nodded. "Yes, after the cherry tree. It symbolizes birth and death, beauty and violence. Your legacy."

"You know nothing about me, let alone my legacy."

The nightmare laughed again. Rissa hated how sweet she sounded. "I know everything that matters about who you are, daughter. The stars, your blood, the bones, the tea leaves. Every single seer I came to told me the exact same thing."

"And what's that? That you're a terrible excuse for a mother?"

"No, daughter. They told me you'll be the bridge between all folk. The wild, the free, the courts. They told me you'd fight for our freedom. And die for it, too."

NIGHTMARES

The blade still in hand, Rissa stared. Did her mother just say she was going to die?

"So, that's your excuse. You saw your kid was going to clock out, and figured you shouldn't bother with it?"

The nightmare was entirely unapologetic. "I sense anger. I can tell it's directed at me. Trust me when I say, you wouldn't have liked being raised by me."

She was certain that this, at least, was the truth.

"Whatever you say. I'll get my friends."

Any excuse to walk away from this...thing.

It dawned on Rissa that she didn't even know her mother's name. Her father had called her Reina, but he'd also explained that was more of a title than a name—whatever nightmare was in charge of their clan was named the reina.

She didn't want to ask her. She didn't want to have anything at all to do with her. If it hadn't been pouring out there, she wouldn't have even considered her offer.

"Hey!" she screamed up to the tree.

Teoran's head popped out of a hammock. Rissa realized that wasn't the one she'd left him in.

"Are you with Khal?"

Teoran giggled.

Giggled.

"We're sharing body heat," he called back cheerfully.

Right. Rissa rolled her eyes. "Get dressed. We have somewhere to stay for the night."

Maybe.

Or maybe they were walking into a trap.

"Here?" Khal yelled from above.

"I'll tell you when you get down."

She waited in defiant silence, playing with the knife in her hand and not looking at the nightmare queen.

Rissa was infuriated to see how much she'd taken after this creature. She didn't look much like her father, so it made sense, but the resemblance was unnerving all the same.

"By the gods!" Teoran said, looking between Rissa and Reina. "Is that—"

"Mother dearest." Her snarl precluded further probing.

Khal, for his part, simply inclined his head in greeting, remaining on his guard.

"Lead the way."

Reina complied without bothering with any more conversation, to Rissa's relief. Every word that woman said set her skin ablaze. The panic and guilt from earlier were entirely gone, replaced by a wall of resentment.

She'd had a good, loving father. Titus could be emotionally and occasionally physically absent, but he'd seen to her needs. She'd been spoiled rotten as a child, given the best education, the best clothing and pretty trinkets. She'd never even paused to think about her mother more than fleetingly. The betrayal and hurt hitting her right now had come out of nowhere, buried deep, at the very core of her psyche.

This was a woman who should have loved her, and didn't. Rissa may not have considered that before, but now that she did, it hurt like a bitch.

"What direction are we going in?" she asked Teoran in a hushed whisper.

He grimaced. "It's harder to tell in the night. I want to say southeast. We're getting a little off course."

She glared at Reina's back. What was her endgame?

"Do you want to talk about the mother thing?" he asked.

"Do you want to talk about the Khal thing?" she shot back, certain Teoran would back down.

He laughed. "What can I say? Adrenaline makes you do stupid things. Besides, it was cold."

"That's all there is to it?" Too bad. She liked the idea of these two together.

Teoran shrugged. "He's certainly handsome enough, and he knows what he's doing, but I'm thirty-one."

She hadn't asked for his age. Thirty-one was six years after the age of majority, but still very young, for a fae. Rissa nodded, understanding him perfectly. He was playing around, not seeking anything serious. The only folk who paired up this early did so because of antiquated betrothals. There were also these who'd found their fated mates, but they were rare.

"Now circling back to your mother. What's the tension about?"

Rissa could feel her shoulders tightening. "This is our first meeting."

Teoran blinked. "Ever?"

She blew a breath out. "I mean, I must have met her vagina at some point, I suppose. She gave me to Titus when I was days old. He always said nightmares aren't naturally motherly. I never questioned it." If this meeting was anything to go by, her father had been right.

"Do you trust her?" Teoran whispered.

"No," she replied automatically. "But I asked her if we'll be safe tonight, and she replied clearly. I want us gone by dawn."

Teoran nodded, sliding to the rear with Khal.

They trekked through mud in the rain, until they reached the flank of a peculiar chain of hills. As they drew closer, Rissa noticed openings in the darkness.

"Caves?" She regretted speaking the moment the word crossed her lip.

"That's the haven," Reina said without further explanation.

They reached one of the openings, and walked into what appeared to be a well-sculpted network of caves, filled to the brim.

Stunned, she watched the gathering before her eyes. There were all sorts of creatures; a family of felines sleeping in a pile, wraiths sliding in the air, imps, goblins, trolls, and worse.

She watched an imp trade a goblin a knife for a haunch of meat . Great spiders the size of horses were weaving, and those who dared approach left them offerings, in exchange for which they received skeins of precious spider silk.

Rissa had never seen a place quite like this. Prey and predators, monsters and saviors coexisted in a strange symbiosis. Out there, there were no rules, but within the confines of these caves, their community worked, somehow. Courtless, these folk were free, but not quite as wild as she would have expected.

"How does this place even work?" Khal mused.

"The rules are simple. No one draws blood here. If anyone breaks this rule, they're fair game." Reina's grin was downright terrifying.

Rissa needed to practice that smile. It'd give Rydekar a fright.

"A smile!" Teoran grinned at her. "That's the first for some hours."

She *was* smiling, to her embarrassment. Despite the events of the day, thinking about the unseelie king was enough for the corners of her lips to lift.

He'd dug his claws deep inside her, in their short acquaintance. Rissa was going to have to do her best to rid herself of the infatuation. He'd take pleasure in playing with her heart strings if she let him.

"It's dry and warm in here." Great fires were burning in each cavernous hall. "Of course I'm smiling."

Reina led the way to a small gathering of nightmares. They were all dark of skin, various shades of blues and green.

"What have we here?"

"It's the child," Reina said dismissively.

She was an *it* now. Curious glances took her

in. As they scrutinized her, Rissa shamelessly did the same to them.

Growing up, she'd assumed that what didn't come from Titus, she'd taken from her unseen mother, but she had to come to terms that these people weren't like her either. Her skin did have a tendency to turn bluish when she was ill, or using too much power, but other than that—and the fact that her face was a copy of Reina's—they had little in common. No one was boasting thorns and vines. No one was covered in feathers. The things that set her apart were all hers; not Titus's, and not Reina's legacy.

"She has good taste in boys," one of the nightmares crooned. Her skin was so dry it looked like it might peel off. She must be ancient, though she remained stunning to behold. "Do you share, child?"

"Sorry, not in my nature." Khal and Teoran weren't hers to share, but they didn't need to know that.

The nightmare cackled. "You're your mother's daughter. She kept that pretty father of yours all to herself, you know."

Rissa winced. She could have lived a long, happy life without hearing that.

"Come. Sit by the fire, child. Your boys may join, too."

Rissa opted to accept the crone's invitation.

"Are there any male nightmares?" she asked out of curiosity.

The crone chuckled. "Of course. Do I need to explain how babies are made?"

She rolled her eyes. "Are they all gone, then?"

One of the nightmares—a long-haired beauty —held a hand up. "I'm male."

"Me too!" another one chimed in.

Khal blinked. "Are you sure?"

Rissa chuckled, but she couldn't blame him. They were all so beautiful and delicate, she'd made the same assumptions.

"Last I checked, yes. I piss upright," the first one announced, quite proudly.

"So, child, what brings you to our parts? Did you come to visit your old lady?" one of them asked, as though it was the most natural thing.

Rissa supposed it might have been, in an alternate reality, where Reina had bothered to get to know her before now.

"Not really." She would have preferred to leave it at that, but all eyes were on her. "I've never been to the Wilderness before. I was curious."

She wasn't sharing her travel plans for all to hear. There may be a truce of sorts within these walls, but there was no telling what would happen after the rain. Besides, friendly as they appeared, she didn't trust the nightmares. They were her mother's people. They could have been hers, but it was a century too late to attempt familial rapport.

"At least you had the sense to come with an escort," the crone said. "You'd get eaten alive here."

She pursed her lips.

"Rissa can take care of herself," Khal said.

"Hm," Reina replied noncommittally. "If you'd like to eat, we have dried meat."

Teoran accepted the offered food readily enough. Khal and Rissa remained silent. She was glad to be out of the storm, but that was the extent of what she'd take from Reina.

Warming up by the fire, Rissa listened to the nine nightmares gossip, never offering more than a word here and there. Teoran fell asleep soon after their arrival, but she and Khal remained vigilant.

"You should sleep," she told him.

"Back at you."

She couldn't. Not here, so close to this stranger.

Her mother had an agenda. Why appear after all this time otherwise?

"It's not natural for nightmares to sleep at night," the crone said to Khal. "That's when we feed."

"Feed?" He tilted his head.

The crone chuckled, moving to stand over Teoran. Her palms hovered over his forehead.

"The boy has demons. He's haunted by faces—many faces. Yes. Delicious nightmares."

They watched as a dark mist came out of Teoran's skin, floating toward her open palms.

He took a deep breath, and broke into a blissful smile.

"You've taken his nightmares?" Rissa guessed.

The crone nodded. "I can feed on dreams too, of course. I'm being nice to your boy so you come back to see us. We don't have many children."

"I'm no longer a child," she felt compelled to remind them.

The nightmare chuckled again. "Girl, I have seen the Old World of the folk. I came to these lands with Mab herself. I beheld the gods before they left us. You're a child to us, and so you will remain for the next thousand years."

Rissa couldn't help a curious glance toward Reina.

"She's older than us, your mother," said another nightmare. "And more patient, too. You'll understand her, one day."

"Am I not supposed to die saving the free world before then?" She could imagine dying before understanding Reina.

The old lady laughed again before returning to her seat, leaving Rissa confused, angry, and frustrated.

FACES

"I wondered whether you'd fall asleep today."

Rydekar sat next to her on the wooden bench, right on the old crone's seat. He smiled down at her, stunning as always.

"I'm asleep?" Her heart raced. "Oh no. How do I stop it?"

He frowned. "Why?"

"I can't be asleep where I am, trust me. I need to—"

"Calm down. I think I can wake you up."

She breathed in and out. Good. "Do it."

"First things first. Earlier today, you were scared. What's going on? Where are you?"

Where did she even start with that? "Khal, he —he almost died. For a moment, I thought he might have."

Rydekar straightened up. She saw his eyes flash with pure rage.

She deserved it; it was her fault. The least she could do was assume the responsibility. "I shouldn't have...I was careless and—"

"He's fine, right?"

She nodded.

"Good. Wake up."

He faded right before her eyes, replaced by her mother's face, standing too close.

"You have interesting dreams."

This woman loved to set Rissa's teeth on edge. "Stay out of my head."

"Hm. That boy of yours. Does he treat you well?"

"Why pretend you're interested?"

Reina gave her question some consideration. "I am curious," she admitted. "Not interested. Now come. Let's talk of this quest of yours."

Rissa's eyes narrowed on her mother's retreating figure.

Khal was asleep, Teoran's head on his lap. She considered waking him up, but opted against it. She could handle Reina.

"You know some have tried to enter the mountain before you and failed, don't you?" Reina asked lightly once they were at the edge of the cave.

The view of the Wilderness in the light of dawn was incomparable. She committed it to memory, wishing she had the skills to draw or paint it to gaze upon it every day.

Rissa hadn't known any such thing, so she shrugged noncommittally.

"You'll manage," Reina stated.

"Thanks for the vote of confidence, I suppose."

Reina's smile had little kindness to it. "It was spelled to keep anyone but those of the line of Mab out."

So she knew she'd get in because of her bloodline—it hadn't been a compliment. Rissa should have guessed.

"Inside, you'll find your prince. I could give you my advice on how to deal with him, but I have a feeling you'd dismiss it."

Reina had that right.

"Instead, I'll tell you one thing. Take the crown."

Rissa couldn't follow that train of thought. "So you want a queen for a daughter, is that it? You realize I'm not likely to give you any favor, I hope." She didn't even mean to be spiteful. If she ever acted as queen, the desires of a stranger wouldn't move her, and that was what Reina was. A stranger. She'd given her somewhere to stay for one night, and this debt, Rissa would repay one day. Beyond that, they had nothing to do with one another.

"I've said my piece. Make of it what you will.

Many among the guests here don't take kindly to strangers. You should wake your friends and go, child."

She didn't need to be told twice.

Riding front and center, Rydekar might seem the picture of composure, but he'd woken agitated and remained so throughout the day.

The glimpse he'd had of Rissa hadn't been comforting. She'd dug herself into some trouble, and considering her distressed, half-baked apology, Khal had paid the consequences.

Had anyone else caused his cousin harm, Rydekar would have taken pleasure in destroying everything they held dear, but it was Rissa. The best he could manage was a stern look, an insult, and maybe a sigh.

The twelve men and women in his personal guard were handpicked, not only for their strength but also their loyalty, to him and to Tenebris, but right then, he would have exchanged every single one of them to have Khal with him, guarding his back as he always did.

Khal was alive. Rissa was alive. He had to concentrate on that. Never mind her horror, when she'd realized she'd dozed off. She wasn't in a safe place.

His concern was unwarranted and ill-advised. Of course she wasn't safe; she was in the Wilderness, risking her life for no good reason. Not that she would have been much safer here. She was the seelie queen. She'd always have enemies. Attempted murders. Poisoning. Not to mention the human scum picking at her unguarded kingdom.

Rydekar was venturing farther than he'd planned into taken territory. He'd passed several deserted cities, villages, settlements, and hadn't yet encountered any human soldiers, though the devastation they left behind was proof of their passage. Where were they hiding?

"Movement from the east!" Penna shouted from the rear.

Blades flashed as all horses swerved to face the direction of the oncoming threat.

"At ease," Rydekar ordered, though his sword remained drawn.

What was this woman doing here?

The Bone Queen rode alone on a red horse, her hair loose in the wind. In a way, she reminded Rydekar of Rissa. If nothing else, both women had a gift for ignoring what they were told. "Don't you have a border to guard?" he shouted when she was within hearing range.

The queen snorted. "Don't you? That didn't stop you from having a bit of fun."

...fun?

"It's a reconnaissance, not a promenade."

"If you think promenades are more fun than reconnaissance missions, I pity your girlfriend."

Rydekar didn't have a girlfriend. He had an irksome mate who'd sent herself on a suicide mission he hadn't stopped.

"I don't need complications with the seelie forces." If Sura died on his watch, the fragile alliance might come to a crashing end. "Go back to your soldiers."

She leaned forward. "Does barking orders usually work?"

It used to.

"You don't know the seelie lands. I do. Clearly, the humans are hiding, and you have no clue where. You need me."

Rydekar sighed.

What had he done for life to throw another seelie queen at him? At least he didn't want to strip this one naked more than he wanted to strangle her.

He considered forcing her to turn back, but paused to weigh his options. "I don't have time to waste. Let's go."

The queen insisted they take a forest path; Rydekar could see the appeal of moving without being seen, but he hadn't thought it wise. She'd been right when she'd pointed out that he didn't know these lands.

Though her own kingdom was east of the

Winter Court through which they now roamed, Sura seemed to know her way.

Too well.

"We'll reach the Winter City from the north, traveling through these woods?"

The queen smiled as she trotted. "We'll be there in less than an hour."

He let her take the lead, hanging back along with his guard.

As they neared a river, she yelled, "We should let the horses drink and rest now—we're almost there."

Rydekar made no protest. They led the horses to the water and dismounted.

None of the horses were interested in the water, except for hers.

"How did you like your queen when you met?" he asked out of genuine curiosity as his guard closed in.

"She's a beauty. A little young to be taken seriously, but smart enough."

"Hm." Rydekar wasn't by nature patient, and this game was getting old. "Now, do you want to tell me who you are, or should I find out the hard way?"

She blinked. "I don't know what you're—"

"How did you get to my men, I wonder?" He tilted his head. "Some have laid down their lives for me in the past, yet you got them to turn against me."

Sura's easy smile slowly morphed into a sneer. Good; the thing was done with pretense. "You don't deserve their loyalty."

Rydekar shrugged. "The hard way it is."

His men were the first to strike. Teyn, the merry jester with a ready laugh, launched at him with a scream, eyes wild. Rydekar evaded his blade, grabbed it with his glove and pulled it. Losing his balance, the knight fell forward. Rydekar swiftly sliced his throat with his hand knife, before tossing it at the thing wearing Sura's face. It dodged the blow, but only just—the line of blood on her cheek showed just how close the hit had been. Augurn and Penna were next, coming at him together, hit after hit. It pained Rydekar to kill the twins, but he did it all the same.

The nine knights left jumped him as one.

COLDER PATHS

They hiked from dawn to late afternoon, eager to put as much space as possible between the caves and them. Who knew what prey the predators would choose to hunt when they awoke? There was a fair chance some were already on their trail, and the last thing any of them needed was another attack.

Walking through woods so thick they appeared dark at the brightest hour of the day, Rissa was stunned when she finally discerned a light ahead. She glanced back to Khal and Teoran. "I think we're here! That's the edge of the forest."

Though Teoran nodded, neither he nor Khal seemed particularly delighted at the prospect.

Rissa practically ran. Despite the cold, soggy boots and the clothes that felt damp and sticky against her skin, her energy was renewed. They were here. They'd made it.

At the edge of the woods, she slowed to a stop. Rissa couldn't believe her eyes. The mountain looked exactly like she would have imagined, a lone peak surrounded by hectares of hard, bare stone, solemn and strangely ominous.

She wondered what truly drove Queen Una to pick this place for her son. Far from the courts and perilous to reach. Why not let him rest in a grand mausoleum, or a castle?

She licked her lips, edging forward.

"I don't like this." Khal shook his head. "This place feels wrong."

"There's magic blocking our way," Teoran added. "I can feel it. And there's nothing breathing there. No animal."

Reina had warned her about it. "It'll let me through," she said. "Can you wait here? I shouldn't be long."

"This is a bad idea." Khal closed his eyes.

"Teoran's right; there isn't even an animal in there. Nothing to harm me. I'll be back in no time."

She stepped forward before they could further discourage her. They were here; they'd made it in one piece. She wasn't about to give up now.

The mountain was a rough, steep climb she didn't look forward to attempting, but as she drew closer, she realized she wouldn't have to: there was a doorway carved at its base. Circular and marked with sigils she couldn't read, it led to a smooth stone staircase leading up and up, and up.

Inside, the mountain was hollow. Its walls shone bright with precious stones, veins of golden dust, and the occasional icicle. The gallery was breathtakingly beautiful. She'd been hasty in assuming this wasn't a mausoleum. Except its inhabitant was alive, somewhere here.

She started the slow ascent up the endless stairs.

If she'd believed the cave was cold at its base, it was nothing to the freezing air higher up, but still she climbed.

She didn't know how long she kept going. After her legs and arms begged her to turn back, after her blood ran cold, after she struggled to breathe, there was finally a light.

She looked back. It was impossible to see the bottom of the stairs from here, but something inside her longed to return there.

Biting her lower lip, she marched into the light.

～

L ong had she heard tales of the cursed prince. She'd seen dozens of paintings and statues in his effigy. None prepared her for him.

Tharsen was said to be beautiful when he was exquisite. They told of his luminous aura, when it was brighter than the northern star in the dead of the night. He was beyond gods and monster, beyond fae and man.

She'd never felt so strong a draw to anyone—anyone at all. Not even Rydekar.

They were kin, he and she. She was the daughter of his second cousin. Yet she was an insignificant sparrow and he, the strongest of eagles soaring the sky. Barely the same species. He was everything she wasn't. The dream to her nightmare.

No wonder people disparaged him. They were envious. They wanted to be him, have him, be noticed by him. One only needed to look at him to fall under a spell.

Yes, he'd do. He'd rule all of Denarhelm, and all would be only too pleased to bow at his feet. They'd crawl to him and demand to serve.

Rissa couldn't deny that the thought terrified her. This creature could bring an end to the free will of the folk, with no more than a glance.

She dared to caress the glass window in the ice coffin encasing him.

Then she stepped back, startled. It felt...alive.

She'd hoped that he would be, of course, but this was beyond slumber, a curse. He felt like he was living, breathing, thinking. Needing. She could feel his pulse beating through the ice. That shouldn't be possible, but she'd left the realm of possibility the moment she entered his prison.

He was a myth come alive. A beautiful prince under a curse.

She supposed that made her the heroine of the story. The brave princess who'd rescue him, so that he may rule and she could return to the shadows, where she belonged.

Her story ended where his would begin.

She would return to the solitary woods she'd claimed as her own, and let the kings of the world play games of war.

Just as she wanted. Everything was right under her grasp.

So why was she hesitating?

Give in. Give in to me.

Yes. Why wouldn't she? He was so very perfect.

Her trembling left hand found its grip on the knife at her side.

Yes. Just a little blood. It won't even hurt.

She closed her eyes.

Everything about him felt familiar. Part of her. As though he'd been with her forever. As though he was right under her skin.

She felt like the unmoving statue didn't like her way of thinking, and by all the gods, she needed to please him. She needed to serve him. And free him.

She sliced the palm of her hand open and pressed it against the glass.

Words she'd never heard, read, thought of, or seen mentioned anywhere crossed her lips in slow, guttural chants. It was her mouth, her vocal cords, her voice. But it wasn't her at all.

Panic gripped her chest. Sheer panic. This didn't feel right at all. The voice urging her forward at every step for days had left her, her need to see this quest accomplished fleeing like it had been nothing but a dream.

She removed her hand from the ice coffin.

"No!" she heard herself scream.

Her hand was slapped right back against the surface.

"Stay right here if you know what's good for you."

The face she saw reflected on the ice was nothing like her; she'd never held such a malevolent sneer.

Her heart beat faster and faster.

This thing was controlling her. It had been for days, if not longer.

Her own mouth curved into a smile. "Oh, don't try to pin that on me. It's not like people didn't try to warn you, princess. You took every step of your own accord. Because you just had to know better, didn't you?" Her laugh felt like a punch to the guts. "Serissa Braer just has to be right, like every other spoiled brat in the world."

"*Let me go.*" She couldn't even get the words out.

Her own face tilted. "But you came so far, darling."

She fought to regain control, to move her hand, to get out of there, but it was hopeless, and useless.

Finally, her hand detached itself from the cold surface. She snatched it back, feeling the burn in her fingertips.

Rissa stared as the ice, solid moments ago, melted away in a fine mist.

There's no shame in being wrong, so long as you can learn from it. There's no shame in retreating to bounce back. There's no shame in growing.

Rydekar had been right about everything else. Hopefully, he was right about that, too.

She raised her knife to Tharsen's chest, aiming for the heart.

THE GOLDEN PRINCE

Blood oozed out of his brow, his every pore, and dropped to the riverbank.

Rydekar spit on the ground, grimacing at the sight of his own blood. He straightened up. "Just you and me, now. Let's see if you still like the hard way."

Sura's doppelgänger had already withdrawn several paces away from him, and though it tried to project the appearance of confidence, it glanced left and right, looking for an exit like any cornered prey.

He stepped over the body of a man he once knew, a man he once valued. A man he'd killed. He was going to have to explain his death to his family. To all of their families. Because of her. It.

The doppelgänger stepped back as he strolled to it. "Oh, no. You don't get to leave now. You and I are going to have a nice chat."

From the first glance, he'd felt something wrong from the creature. While it had Sura's scent, as well as all her physical features, the nonchalant, commanding woman didn't talk like that creature. Sura wouldn't have left her soldiers behind, either, from what he'd gathered at their first meeting. The last straw was what it had said about Rissa. A smart, young beauty who couldn't be taken seriously? While all three things were true enough, they were the last adjectives anyone who'd actually met her would have used about Serissa. Impulsive. Full of life. Unstoppable. Compassionate. Commanding. All that came before anything else. Her youth, her beauty, and her intelligence were the least of her numerous strengths.

"Who are you?"

It just snarled.

Rydekar summoned his compulsion ability, throwing it at the thing without tempering any of its strength, hitting it full on. "Who. Are. *You.*"

The creature screamed, resisting the compulsion with all its might.

Which, as it turned out, wasn't much. The illusion the double was hiding under flaked like cheap paint on glass, flying in the wind. Rydekar stood, staring at none other than Siobhe.

He had to admit a certain degree of confusion. Of all those he might have suspected of concocting something like this, she might have been last. Not that he didn't believe her to be arrogant or malicious enough for it, but she certainly was no mastermind.

"Oh, Siobhe. I feel like I should ask why." And he might have, if he cared for an explanation.

She showed her perfect little teeth, a kitten growling at a tiger. "You humiliated me. You humiliated me, and brought the child you left me for before the courts."

He was right. She wasn't behind anything. She'd been recruited after Rissa's arrival—perhaps even after the poisoning.

"Who made you take Sura's place?" His voice was entirely void of emotion, because he felt nothing at her treason. Not so much as a tinge of betrayal. Siobhe was no one to him. He'd wed her, as was his duty, and he had bedded her once, to make the union legal under the fairy laws, but there were servants and courtesans he'd fucked more than his former wife.

"Fuck you."

Rydekar sighed. He wasn't going to enjoy hurting her. Pulling the wings off hapless butterflies was a game he'd grown tired of long ago.

All the same, he lifted his hand and Siobhe rose, levitating away from the ground. Her hands went to her throat, thrashing to fight against his invisible hold, to no avail.

He crushed her throat harder. "Who, Siobhe?

One name. That's all I'm asking. Then your suffering can end."

She sobbed, never one used to any form of discomfort.

A better man might have been moved by tears.

Finally, she gave him one name.

He waved his hand and her corpse fell on the snowy ground, neck broken in two places.

Rydekar snarled.

He should have seen this coming.

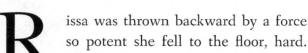

Rissa was thrown backward by a force so potent she fell to the floor, hard. She leaped to her feet, and immediately regretted the haste. Her ankle could barely take any weight. Broken, or at least sprained.

Ignoring the pain shooting through her limbs, she looked around for her knife.

Alarm sparked inside her when she found it in the grasp of a long, cold hand.

Tharsen was even more stunning now, standing beyond the ice coffin, but his eyes held no life, no warmth. Nothing at all.

She glanced backward. "Oh, I think not. It's far too late for that, my darling cousin." His voice was sweet as syrup, in contrast to the coldness of his still gaze.

Instinctively drawing backward, she winced at her first step, but she took another, and another all the same.

Tharsen chuckled low in his throat.

"What do you want from me?" To her relief, her voice held more strength than fear, though fear was blurring her vision, making her want to vomit, scream, and run all at once.

"Nothing." He glanced back at the empty coffin behind them. "You got me out of that mess. I should thank you. And I might have, too, had you not gotten unnecessarily stabby."

His vernacular threw her; it seemed uncharacteristically modern, for a man who'd spent the last few thousand years in a box. Even her father didn't talk like that.

But he hadn't truly been in a box, had he? He'd lived. Through her mind, her eyes. Who knew who else he'd been able to manipulate?

"Don't give me too much credit. My power only extends to our dear grandmother's line."

"Didn't I tell you to stay out of my head?"

"What was it that your boy said?" His smile was cruel. "Make me."

He seemed to like hearing himself talk. Distasteful as the thought might be, Rissa opted to let him, if only to gain some time.

"How did you do it? Make me come here," she clarified.

Seemingly pleased with the inquiry, Tharsen

smirked. "You wanted to *help,* without having to shoulder any responsibility. I only had to plant a teensy bud of a thought. You did the rest."

She would have loved to be able to contradict him, but she had been desperate to find a way out of the fate Rydekar proposed. And this was where she'd headed, despite everything he'd told her, despite all her own misgivings.

"I had doubts," she said.

"I erased them. Easier than it might have been, had you not been so busy rationalizing your relationship with that boy." The prince shook his head, his perfect curls bouncing under the crown at his brow. "You're such a blind, wistful child with so many mommy issues, you couldn't even recognize your own mate."

Rissa froze as Tharsen sauntered to her. "I pity him. He gazed upon you and saw nothing. No recognition. No reason to care. No wonder he let you run to your death."

"No." She didn't know what she was protesting against. Everything. Nothing at all. She shook her head for good measure.

Tharsen was wrong. He had to be. She couldn't be—she couldn't have a mate. She'd know if she did.

The prince lifted his unnervingly long finger till he reached her temple, almost caressing her cheek. "I told you I could see the line of Mab. Even its most degenerate members, it seems."

Without any other cue, he hit her with a thousand different visions, images she could barely make sense of. Feelings, voices, whispers, dreams, and nightmares.

Over the dizzying chatter, Rissa identified her father's voice. *"Rydekar Bane, my daughter Serissa."*

Now that she'd managed to find a point of focus, the pace of the visions slowed and formed around her. Suddenly, she wasn't so cold anymore. She wasn't at the top of a forbidden mountain with a monster. She was in Volderas, during her fifteenth winter.

Only she wasn't herself. The mind wrapping around her wasn't hers. It was too steady, too organized, in neat boxes. A seelie mind. The kind of mind she'd never had although she was born in Denarhelm. Everything was simple and logical and working according to a set of priorities. At the very top came Charlotte Bane, the person's mentor and parental figure. He had a mother and a father, but both had more or less abandoned him to the care of his grandmother the queen, who raised him to rule. But just as she inhabited this mind at the very moment, it was reorganizing itself. To hell with the will of the queen. To hell with everything. The only thing that mattered to this person, in that very moment, was Serissa. The woman made for him.

He bowed to her, lower than he'd ever bowed

to any living woman. She was too young then, but he promised himself. Soon.

He'd come to her soon.

A cruel, detached laugh pulled her from the dream. "Wasn't that sweet?"

Rissa blinked into the beautiful face of Prince Tharsen. Sweet? "It was a lie. It never happened."

The prince rolled his eyes. "Tell yourself whatever you wish. I don't suppose it matters in the end."

The end? The end of what?

But both of his hands had reached out for her throat now, and his ravishing face contorted into a terrifying mask as his now-amethyst eyes flashed with need.

Something—something deep inside her, that belonged to no one but her—was pulled to the surface, dragged out of her skin, and stripped away.

Rissa screamed, and screamed, and screamed, until darkness claimed her.

THE PRICE

Rissa was startled when she blinked awake. Not because she didn't know where she was. She'd genuinely expected never to open her eyes again. And part of her knew she might just deserve that fate.

After however long she'd spent passed out on the icy cold floor of the cavern, she'd accepted several painful facts. Firstly, she'd released a monster upon Denarhelm and the rest of the world. Sure, it had manipulated her into it, but at the end of the day, the guilt still belonged to her.

Secondly, she was a foolish, blind, stupid child, who'd missed out on the best thing that could ever have happened to her, out of pride. Pride and self-preservation. She'd been scared of the draw between herself and Rydekar. Scared enough to embrace a journey, so long as it took her away from him as fast as possible.

Not that he'd tried to hang on to her, but still. She believed Tharsen. What cause would he have to lie? He was winning. He'd achieved everything he wanted. He now was free, and the crown of her kingdom was his for the taking.

Her kingdom.

She crawled to her feet, relieved to find herself alone at first.

"You're already awake? Wonderful. I'm glad you took so well to it. You're quite an exquisite meal, cousin."

Though there had been no one around her moments ago, Tharsen now sat back against his coffin, tossing her knife in the air.

"What did you do to me?"

He sighed. "I suppose paying attention was never your forte. That's called siphoning. Your friend told you about my ability, didn't he?"

This slug had honestly sucked out all her thoughts for days. She grimaced.

"You should have believed him. For the record, however, siphons don't tend to kill those they absorb if they can help it. Why waste a good source of energy? I'll see that you remain cared for and pampered in between feedings."

"You're a monster." How could he think doing something like that to another living, breathing, sentient being was all right?

"And you're a brunette. Can we move on to something new?"

"Are you going to kill me?" she asked.

"No can do. Your blood destroyed the seal," Tharsen reminded her. "If you died without my lifting that curse of mine, there's a chance I'd end up stuck back into that box, at best. Dead, maybe. I don't want to find out."

Good, he was done with her. Rissa tested her foot, and while it certainly had seen better days, her fae blood did give her a faster healing rate, for which she was grateful. She could put some weight on it.

She moved to take the stairs.

A chuckle followed her, but she ignored it, taking a step, then another, as fast as she could.

Without notice, Tharsen appeared right in front of her. "Where do you think you're going?"

"You got what you wanted." Her teeth flashed. "You're out of your prison, and you took... whatever you took from me."

"Your psychic energy—what you use to call to your magic." He chuckled again. "And if you think you're going anywhere, you're mistaken. You taste wonderful."

He leered at her, and she felt her stomach churn. If she read him right, and he was interested in sucking more than some weird metaphysical thing out of her, she was going to actually vomit.

"Don't pout. We'll be perfect, you and I. I'm as seelie as they come, and wherever you were born, I've never sampled such an unseelie soul. Our dynasty will rule the fairy realm for eternity."

Bile rose in her throat. "You're my cousin."

"Well, I'm your father's nephew actually," he argued. "Our children may just be sound of mind."

With him as a father? Unlikely. "I'd die before I let you touch me."

That laugh again. So sweet, melodious and full of life. Gifts like his should never have landed in the hands of the devil. "I love that you think you have a choice in the matter."

But she did. She knew she did in that moment, more than she'd ever known anything in her life.

Because someone had told her so. Someone had told her exactly how this story was going to go.

It wasn't the ending she'd wanted when she'd set out for the north. But in a wrapped-around way, she was getting what she'd craved.

Rissa had wanted to be the hero, the one who helped her country without ordering it about. A knight out of a fairy tale written for mortal children.

Maybe she was only saving them from her own mistake, and no one would hear of it. But all the same, her actions were going to be for the good of the realm.

Rydekar would be proud.

They told me you'll be the bridge between all folk. The wild, the free, the courts. They told me you'd fight for our freedom. And die for it, too.

She'd been ready to dismiss everything out of Reina's mouth out of spite. That woman had abandoned her. What did she know or care of Rissa's fate?

But perhaps Reina, like Rydekar, and all those who shouldered the burden of caring for their subjects, had done what she'd believed was best for the good of all when she'd handed her to her father. Perhaps she'd known it would come to this one day. That Rissa was going to be the one to wake Tharsen, and that she was the one who'd be able to end it for good.

She glanced backward, over the wide staircase, to the drop.

"What are you doing?"

She didn't think. She couldn't think—her thoughts weren't hers, not while he was able to invade them. She brought the easiest image her mind could conjure. His. Rydekar's, the first time she'd seen him in her clearing. Then, back at her father's court. His smirk. His expression when he'd danced with her. The sensation he brought to her core when he touched her, oh so innocently, barely grazing her skin.

She took a step back, and let herself fall.

"No!"

Tharsen moved to catch her, but she was also fae, and as swift as he when she wished it. His hand reached out for her. She had to admit her weaker instinct was to take it. Hang on to her life, maybe get to experience a little more of it.

But her mother had been right. Rydekar had been right.

For this single moment as she fell to her death, she was the seelie high queen. Noble, powerful, and ruthless to the enemies of the folk. Crownless though she may be, she was ruling.

Take the crown.

Three words she'd also dismissed, like everything else that had truly mattered, but they resonated through her mind just as Tharsen bent forward. She reached for the gaudy crown he wore, and found it just a hair out of her grasp.

Rissa closed her eyes, resigned, attempting to find one last moment of peace.

It never came.

Though her fall stopped, Rissa found no crushing pain, no slow crawl to death.

She dared to crack one eye open, then gasped, and stared at the thing floating in front of her, held by one floating briar vine.

The prince's crown. She would have sworn that was it, though mere moments ago it had been a complex silver and diamond affair with several hanging pendants. Now, it was but one circlet, with a single teal heart stone shining at its centre.

That metamorphosis might have been enough to stun her, if she hadn't already been completely astounded to find herself flying. *Flying.* The useless feathers on her shoulders had extended into strong wings, batting with incredible force.

"You bitch of a thief!"

The scream got her to focus back on her *dear cousin.*

Tharsen practically fell off the stairs in his attempt to catch it, but he wised up, stepping back, fear evident in his silver eyes.

The first thing she noticed was the fear. Then, there was pure hatred. She ignored both, trying to focus on what she saw before her eyes. He'd dimmed. In beauty, in strength, in charisma. Everything about him was now inconsequential. Worthy of little to no notice.

Then she understood. The crown.

The power she'd seen wasn't inside Tharsen. It belonged to his crown.

"This is Mab's crown," she breathed in shock.

The crown of the real high queen, the one who'd stood above seelie and unseelie alike, shaping their realms, their customs, their truth.

"It's *mine!*" Tharsen roared.

Rissa laughed. Was it? "You're a grandson of

Mab. I'm her granddaughter. The way I see it, it could belong to either of us." But she was the one with it at her fingertips. And she'd never let it go again.

Her branches slithered along her skin, bringing her crown to her grasp.

She'd always liked pretty, shiny things and this one was the most precious she'd ever beheld. She set it on her head, before Tharsen's terrified, desperate eyes.

And then she felt it all.

Everything.

Ants crawling underground, imps in the hills, dwarves in their mountains, dragons guarding their treasures, and pirates approaching the coast from the treacherous seas.

Everything was at her fingertips. It all belonged to *her*.

"You took your grandmother's crown upon her death," Rissa stated, seeing it all through his eyes, through his memories. "You stole Mab's legacy. And once it was upon your head, no one could take it." The crown could only be passed down voluntarily. There was a hiccup though—one Tharsen hadn't thought of, or he would have gutted her where she stood.

She'd freed him with her blood, binding them in a way neither of them quite understood.

Enough for the crown to accept her as part of

him. As someone who had as much right to the crown as he. "So they banished you."

"They had no right!" Tharsen snarled.

She laughed. The jury was out on that. "They ensured no one could get to you other than your own blood. For years, you infested the minds of the younger ones of us, attempting to crawl your way in, but they were never desperate enough to think of freeing you."

Until her. He hadn't targeted her by chance; her abandonment issues and desperation to fit into a world not built for the likes of her had played a great part in his success, though her naivety was equally guilty.

"If you don't give it back to me—"

She didn't stay to hear the rest of his threat. He was an enemy. Perhaps an enemy she should have taken the time to eliminate, but crownless or not, Tharsen was a warrior who would have fought tooth and nail, and time was one luxury she didn't have.

She instinctively directed those beautiful, strange wings of hers to let her drop to the bottom of the mountain, and exited her cousin's prison the way she'd come in.

Khal and Teoran were arguing at the edge of the woods. She landed before them, more awkwardly than she would have liked. The new wings hadn't come with a manual.

They both took in her haggard appearance, or the crown, or the wings—she couldn't quite tell.

Rissa was fairly certain she would have been able to work it out, had she wished to, but invading people's thoughts without their approval was one ability she fully intended to reserve for foes.

"Wings," Teoran finally said.

"Well, I did have feathers," she pointed out.

She hadn't expected wings in a long time. Natural abilities had a tendency to burst out during a fae's teen years, and she'd never so much as felt the graceful limbs. "I don't think I can carry you, but I need to get to Rydekar." She knew it, as well as she knew that her name was Serissa. "Tharsen is still in the mountain. You were right. He's a monster. I hate to leave you to deal with it..."

"Go," Khal replied. "We're right behind you."

She gathered him in her arms, holding on tightly. The wings moved to encompass Teoran in the bear hug. "Come back in one piece."

After a last look at her friends, she took to the air.

OF LAND AND SEA

Rydekar didn't take many things for granted. Not his crown. Not his people. Not his friends. The only person he was fairly sure of was Khal, and he even occasionally questioned his cousin's loyalty.

Then Rissa had entered his life, and he'd known everything he'd survived, everything he'd endured was going to be worth it, because fate had rewarded him with a mate.

A *mate*. How many folk could say as much? One out of ten thousand, a hundred thousand? But he had her, and nothing could take her away from him.

Yet, just a week before Rissa reached her majority he was called to his grandmother's side. Charlotte invited every lower king and queen in the realm to witness her giving her crown to him.

Him, not his father.

He remembered that very day, a day he might have looked forward to as a small, useless boy. But as the crown was forced on his head, he knew one thing. He had to let her go.

Rissa was young—too young for him, but he would have made it work. He wasn't the first two-hundred-year-old with a twenty-five-year-old mate. He would have been patient, befriended her until she felt their connection. He would have courted her until she saw nothing but him. But he was now high king, with a target on his back, and he had no intention of bringing a pure, innocent soul into the unseelie court.

The plan was simple. Wait a hundred years until Charlotte was satisfied enough to go on her journey to the Eternal Realms, where so many of his ancestors already dwelled, then pass the crown down; ideally to Khal, or one of his cousins, for all he cared.

But war had come to their lands, delaying his agenda again.

A war that had been nothing but a lie.

He should have seen it. He should have questioned everything years ago.

Rydekar rode at the head of his army, along with the seelie contingent. They were after blood, same as him.

They crossed the border of the Court of Sunlight, and rode past Rissa's Darker Woods, before reaching the edge of the Old Keep.

Rydekar was controlled, calculating, careful in all things. Yet, he'd dropped his guard once in the last decade. Just once.

For a pair of big, pretty eyes.

The frozen lake around the keep had been thawed, and virulent waves crashed against the shores, overflowing the bridge with water. In the depth of the dark waters, sharp-toothed selkies and sirens watched them, grinning at the prospect of a fresh meal.

To say that the Old Keep had been taken would misplace the blame. No, he'd handed it to Havryll.

The servant of the High Sea Queen, Nyla.

Imagining that a child so young could rule courts wilder, darker than his—and had done so since her first breath, communicating her orders telepathically—was mind boggling, but he knew it for a fact now. Not only because of Siobhe's confession; he'd managed to track and torture enough ensorcelled victims of her wiles to be certain.

Nyla had released members of the Sea Land Courts into Denarhelm, wearing human sigils, sowing false trails. Through spells and potions released in the wells, she'd controlled the weaker souls of her courts, like a spider carefully weaving her net for years until she was ready to feast on her prey.

She'd chosen the wrong quarry.

"How do we get back to the keep?" the real Sura asked.

To say that the queen was pissed that a woman like Siobhe had used her identity to attempt to trick him was putting it mildly. The trail of curses that had flown out of her mouth would have made a sailor blush.

"Do we have to?" Gaulder shrugged. "If she's isolated out there, what does it matter?"

"It matters because all of the unseelie lords, ladies, and most of the folk who wished to come to safety are in there with her. And so are plenty of seelie fae," Rydekar stated through gritted teeth.

"And we need to kill the bitch."

He nodded at Sura. That, too.

Reaching the keep wouldn't be easy, with a mile of sea separating them from its island.

"We have company."

A dozen archers drew their bows toward the oncoming shadow. It was too large for a bird, too fast for Morgan or any of her air spies.

Rydekar frowned. "Stand down." He couldn't quite make sense of what his squinting eyes were telling him, but the words spilled out nonetheless.

Fast—faster than should have been possible— the creature landed right at his side, wings curved around her body, hitting the ground so hard his horse bucked.

Rissa.

Only this wasn't his Rissa. This wasn't the girl who'd gone north mere days ago. Her clothes were drenched with blood and sweat; her boots, muddy; her skin, dirty and scraped in places. She'd been hurt, cut, broken. More than that, she'd been changed.

Freed.

She wore a crown like she was born to it, without pride, without noticing it, without mistaking it as a reward when it was a duty, a burden.

This was the seelie queen. His mate. His equal, light to his darkness, fire to his steel.

She reached her hand out to him wordlessly. Taking it, he helped her mount his grumpy horse.

Rissa pressed her lips against the skin of his cheek, fleetingly, for the briefest of instants, and all his pain and fatigue disappeared.

"Forward," she ordered, not bothering to raise her voice.

Rydekar obeyed. The unseelie army obeyed. The seelie folk listened to their ruler, and marched upon the open lake.

Rydekar was the first to reach it. His horse's hooves hit a solid surface he couldn't even see under the waves. He stared over his horse's back.

Roots. Tree roots twisted and curled—so many of them, where from, he couldn't tell.

"You must have had an interesting few days."

She laughed over the brouhaha. "You have no idea."

He wanted to hear every single thing, but now wasn't the time. He asked the only question that mattered, now that he could see she was all right with his own eyes. "Khal?"

"He was hurt—he took a lance through a leg, but he healed fast enough. I had to leave him at the forbidden mountain, though. With Tharsen." She winced. "You were right all along, about so many things. He was psychotic. He wanted to keep me locked up like a pet, occasionally suck power out of me, and oh—as if that wasn't bad enough—make babies with me, too."

Rydekar's fists tightened on the reins, but his tone was light. "He sounds like a man of good sense. Locking you up isn't the worst of ideas."

She slapped the back of his shoulder without much heat.

"How did you get away?" he asked over the violent clash of waves.

The sea was doing its best to hinder their path, but Rissa's roots violently twirled to the coast, despite the strength of the current.

"I stole Mab's crown," she yelled back. "I think Tharsen might have let me."

Rydekar had a number of follow-up questions, but they were approaching the shores of the keep.

He would have expected to find the gates

barricaded upon their arrival, but they were wide open, though not one guard, not one soldier defended the outer ward.

His steed cantered the paved street leading up to the motte, growing tenser as they encountered no one in their path.

"Where are they?" Rofrakan's ifrits were marching behind, with the rest of the Court of Ash, but the commander rode with Rydekar.

The Old Keep was built on an island; there was nowhere for thousands of fae to go. Unless they'd been taken underwater.

"Inside the Keep," Rydekar guessed. "Mab built it to be impenetrable. Havryll knows that."

Quieting the rage inside his chest was no small feat. He'd trusted Havryll. The man had climbed in his esteem in the last decade. Rydekar kept almost no secrets from him, and this was his reward?

Part of him wondered what had convinced him of Havryll's loyalty. His great aunt's introduction? The man's efforts? But no—if he was truthful, it had been Nyla.

Havryll had walked in with a beautiful, bright, vulnerable toddler, and Rydekar had immediately bonded with the child.

A child he was going to have to kill.

SEA SALT

"So, there were no Antheosans on land? All along, it was Sea Land soldiers, disguised as humans?" Rissa wrinkled her nose.

No wonder she'd been so confused when she'd smelled the piles of scorched corpses in Deanon and hadn't identified human stench.

"Why would they do this? Don't you have an alliance with them, Rye?"

"There are several courts in the Sea Lands. We're allied with *some* of them. As for why—I suppose you could ask Havryll, if you manage a word with him before I tear his tongue out."

Rissa wasn't surprised to find the keep's doors sealed shut. She huffed a breath, eyes scaling up the stone walls. "We could climb to the bartizan?"

Dismounting his horse, Rydekar picked up a stone and threw it at the wall. It bounced away inches from it, and was projected back with considerable force.

"There's a reason I moved the courts here. No one can walk in once the front doors are sealed."

Rissa bit her lip. That didn't sound right. The Old Keep was brimming with old fae magic. She couldn't believe her ancestors would simply build doors they could be locked out of.

She climbed off the steed and approached the doors, hand extended.

"Wait!" Sura called. "You'll hurt yourself."

Maybe. "I don't think so. I'm wearing Mab's crown. I'm her granddaughter. This place is home."

A part of her had felt it before she'd even reached the island. That knowledge had been floating around the edge of her mind since she'd first seen the keep over the frozen lake. She glanced to Rydekar. "I have to try."

She couldn't quite read him, but finally, a smile tugged at his lip. "We," he declared. "The Old Keep recognizes no court. It stands for all of the folk on land. We do this together."

Rissa nodded, offering a hand he entwined with his, then both of them advanced to the great iron doors, which opened before they'd reached the top step.

On the other side, a nightmare awaited.

Bodies littered the dark great hall. Dozens

upon dozens of dead folk, seelie and unseelie alike. Little folk, great noble gentry, their humble servants; all had seen their end, and bled on the smooth hardwood floor.

Rissa and Rydekar both unsheathed their swords and lifted them at the ready before striding inside. She attempted to avoid the bodies at first, but it affected her balance, so she mirrored Rye, who stepped on the fallen when he had to.

As the rest of their company joined them, Rydekar gestured to the archways leading out. The thick decorative curtains that had been wide open during her previous stay were drawn over the openings, plunging the room into near darkness.

Rissa's eyes could see well enough during the night, like most fae, but the sea folk thrived in obscurity, used to the shadows of the depth of the ocean.

One of Rydekar's men obeyed, and the moment the first curtain twitched, she spotted a figure at the end of the hall.

"Rye." She tilted her chin forward.

Following her look, Rydekar watched the lone man with narrowed eyes.

The stranger seemed familiar, though Rissa strained to realize why at first. There was something in his eyes, the shape of his mouth, and even his stature. Suddenly, she pinpointed where she'd seen it before. On Rydekar.

This man was a washed-out version of Rydekar. Shorter but broader, he had lighter hair than the unseelie king, but other than that, they could pass for brothers.

"Dorin," Rye spat.

She had to think for a moment; she'd heard that name before, but where?

"What, no *Daddy*?" The man laughed. "I'm hurt."

This was Rydekar's father, then.

"No father of mine would betray Tenebris for the Sea Lands."

Dorin's amethyst eyes flashed, but his smile just broadened. "Yeah, well, Tenebris betrayed me first. You were given the crown I was born to wear. I'm simply taking it back."

"If you think the Sea Lands would let you control Tenebris, you're an idiot." Rye's chuckle held no humor. "Never mind. You're an idiot in any case."

Dorin smirked. "What does that make you, son?"

Before Rydekar could open his mouth, the doors slammed shut behind them. At their feet, water started to pool, raising inch by inch at every second.

Dorin laughed, turned on his heels, and left the entry hall.

Crap.

Letting go of Rydekar's hand, Rissa ran forward, willing her wings to spread. It was like stretching an overused, unwilling muscle, but they reluctantly rose at her call. She leaped up, flapping them hard.

Dorin winced, grunting as he attempted to close the heavy door behind him.

Rissa reached it just as his face was about to disappear. He grinned victoriously.

Her wing shot between the closing door and the wall as he shut it.

She screamed, sharp pain shooting down nerve endings she never knew she had. It was worse than breaking a bone. "Fuck!" she yelled, bending in two under the pain.

The water had reached knee level.

Rydekar, already at her side, ran a hand up her back. "It takes time, but wings can heal." He looked grimly at their legs. "So long as we don't drown. Is the door spelled?"

Rissa managed a half smile. "Maybe. Good thing I'm on the other side."

One of Rydekar's eyebrows wiggled, but she was too busy trying to direct her vines to the handle.

It took several tries, as she couldn't see what she was doing, but the door finally unlatched.

Her limp wing bent behind her back, vines

curling around it in an attempt to hold its broken bone in place.

"Looks like it hurts like a bitch," the Bone Queen said, tossing her a deep golden flask.

"A healing potion?" Rissa uncorked it.

Sura shook her head. "Whiskey."

That would do. She sipped some of the amber liquid inside before handing it back. Rydekar intercepted it, and finished off the rest.

They set off after Dorin, empty hall after empty hall, finding nothing but dark rooms and the occasional corpse, until they finally reached the great throne room where Rydekar held his court.

The immense room, also curtained off, was packed; most of the members of court and tons of lower folk had been gathered here. They sat close together, hands bound, while warriors marked by the Sea Land sigil patrolled between their ranks, weapons at the ready.

Rissa snarled, eyes set on the two thrones. Hers and Rydekar's.

A pale child with sea-green braids and coral eyes was occupying hers, and Dorin sat next to her. Between them, Havryll stood, a hand on the child's shoulder.

She wore a dark stately robe, and a red crown too big for her small head.

"I'm glad you're here." The child's voice was clear as crystal and just as cold. "We can talk of where these little kingdoms of yours are heading, going forward." The child stood. "My husband, Dorin, will rule in my name when I'm away. You'll kneel to me and answer to the Sea Lands, or your end will be that of those who defied me. You met some of them on your way in."

And to think Rissa had believed Tharsen was psychotic.

"Your husband?" Rydekar grimaced. "You're nine, Nyla."

He knew the little girl, then.

The little girl laughed. "I was born before Mab, before any of you. I *am* the sea."

He shook his head in disbelief. "You're delusional. And you!" He pointed to his father. "How can you do this? She's a *child*. Has your thirst for power taken whatever honor you might have had left?"

Dorin didn't grace him with an answer.

"I would have preferred it to be you," Nyla said. "But you never seemed interested. Now, I see why." The coral eyes narrowed on Rissa, as though she were an interloper.

"I'm not interested because you're *nine*. And insane."

"Enough. Kneel or die," the child said, almost bored.

"The seelie lands will never answer to the sea!" Sura replied.

"Nor the unseelie kingdom," one of Rye's men added.

The child sighed. "Fine."

Never one to let an enemy land the first blow, Rissa launched herself forward, Rye in her wake.

She'd only crossed half the distance to the dais when she stumbled, her body convulsing in pain. Her chest. Something in her chest was being crushed, twisted, squeezed. Her ears rang and her head was burning up. She fell to her knees. Next to her, Rydekar was doubled over, screaming. Or perhaps the screams came from her, she couldn't tell.

She was dying. The little girl had done something to her—to both of them—and it was killing them fast.

A wave of nausea hit, so strong she could only retch. Blood spilled out of her mouth.

All her strength was leaving her, replaced by a burning pain.

"I'm flooding your king and queen's lungs with salt water, if you're wondering. Kneel, or be next," Nyla demanded.

She didn't know whether the lords obeyed. If they did, they were smart. She would have done just about anything to end this suffering.

Rissa's hand reached for Rydekar's. Through her tears, she could barely see him, but she felt it when his fingers clasped around hers.

At least they were together at the end.

SMOKE AND MIRRORS

Once, there was a nightmare who made a deal with a king. The king was old and heirless. The nightmare was older yet, and had a mind to build a legacy.

Titus Braer fulfilled his end of the bargain, disappearing when the time came for the world to need a leader. He knew Rissa would have been keen to reject the crown if he was there to take the burden. In this, they were alike, seeing power as a responsibility with few advantages. Watching his child stumble from the shadows had been painstaking, but every day away from the wood where she'd hidden, she'd blossomed into a greater woman.

"How is she doing?" Titus's closest friend asked.

Looking away from the enchanted mirror he

used to keep track of Rissa, Titus smiled at Meda. "Dying."

Meda tilted her head. "And we're all right with that?"

Titus brought his wine goblet to his lips. "What's life without a little death?"

His friend rolled her eyes.

Titus returned to the mirror.

"Get up."

∽

"**G**et up."

Two words, in a voice so familiar and comforting it brought more tears to her eyes.

She wanted to obey her father, but she couldn't. It was just too painful.

"Get the hell up, cousin."

Rissa blinked, confused now. That voice she recognized too, but it was certainly not her father's. What she didn't understand was why she heard it here and now.

She was stunned to find that she could see, her vision less blurry, despite the tears. The pain was subsiding. She dragged her sleeve over her eyes.

A hand was extended in front of her, long and pale.

Tharsen's. He was here, the fancy cloth of his cloak floating inches away from her face.

He was here. Was she dead already, or imagining things? She'd left Tharsen in the forbidden mountain, miles north, and she would have been happy never to hear or see him again. Imagining him as she died was strange—and salacious.

The cursed prince had one hand lifted in Nyla's direction, and the other lowered to help her up.

Rissa just stared, half expecting it to turn into a vicious snake. "What are you doing here?"

"I told you."

She was fairly certain he hadn't.

"It's you and me now. You die, I die—or get stuck again. I don't want to find out which, remember?"

Rissa shifted to her knees and crawled to Rydekar. He lay flat on the floor. She checked his pulse, and breathed out in relief when she found it. It was weak, but he was alive.

"My shield won't last, and I can't control her for long," Tharsen said impatiently. "Are you ready?"

Fear coiled in her stomach. If Tharsen stopped whatever he was doing, Nyla would end them. Her power was too deadly. "Ready for what?"

"I can take care of the girl, but I need more power."

He wanted to siphon her again. Rissa snarled. "If you think I'm letting you—"

Tharsen rolled his eyes. "Help me or die. Those are your two choices."

Rissa looked at Rydekar again. What would he do?

The answer came automatically. Everything in his power, for the good of the realm.

If that was how she could help, then so be it.

She got to her feet and took the crazy prince's hand.

"Mirror my position. You need to aim for her —nothing else, understood?"

She frowned, but followed his directives, one hand extended toward Nyla.

"What now?"

"Now you let go. Everything inside you. All your power."

Everything?

Rissa rarely even scratched the surface of her abilities. She didn't know what she was capable of. She'd never been tempted to find out.

She could feel a burning wave of magic emanate from Tharsen's hand. Filaments of gold waved around his hands, his face, lighting up his skin. She knew this magic, soft and nurturing sometimes, but also harsh and unforgiving. She'd felt it on her face, and under her skin.

Rissa had never known how to access this power inside her, but as it came out of Tharsen, she instinctively connected to hers, copying him like an echo.

There it was, burning so hot she hesitated before calling it.

Rissa let go of Tharsen, and both of them lifted their free hands to join the one pointed at the sea queen.

Then there were screams, and fire.

~

Rydekar woke to the sound of screams. Jumping to his feet, ready to launch himself between danger and those he'd sworn to protect, he lifted his sword, only to lower it when the smoke dissipated.

The dais was on fire, thrones burning, but there was no one on it.

All of the sea soldiers had also disappeared.

Mere paces away, Rissa stood next to a stranger, glowering.

What was going on?

"How did you get here?" she asked between gritted teeth.

The man shrugged. "We're linked, you and I. I'll always know where you are. You could also find me, if you so wished."

"I'll never wish to find you. You're a psycho."

He laughed. "Well, either way, we're stuck together, cousin."

Who was he, and why was he so familiar with *his* mate?

He closed the distance. "I missed something." Rydekar looked between the two of them.

"This is Tharsen," she practically spat. "He came to help because I freed him—if I die, he's in danger." To Tharsen, she said, "You'd better not have harmed Khal and Teoran. If you have..."

"Then what, cousin?" he laughed, turning on his heels. "You and I both know you don't have it in you to kill me."

Before Rissa could say a word, Tharsen vanished like he was nothing but an illusion.

THE DANCE

Two hundred and nine. That was the number of bodies they burned three days after the attack.

Two hundred and nine fae of the lands, killed by the sea. They'd pay for their effrontery. Rissa would make sure of it.

She presided over the pyre, wearing a black dress, as was the custom for seelie funerals. Rydekar stood next to her, dressed in white. Hand in hand, they sang for the souls of the fallen. They sang until her voice was hoarse and broken. They sang along with the folk of every kingdom.

Finally, it was time to return inside the keep.

"Your Highnesses!" A dainty winged fae rushed to catch up with them.

Recognizing Morgan, Rydekar's master of spies, Rissa waited. "Well?"

She'd sent her on a critical mission. Ordering an unseelie fae had seemed strange, but Rydekar had told her his men were at her disposal. Her own high court wasn't organized yet, and she barely knew any of the lords and ladies of her own realm, so she'd taken the offer.

Morgan beamed at them. "We spotted them. They're halting at the Autumn Court, but they're both safe."

Rissa smiled back. Teoran and Khal's fate was one of many reasons why she couldn't manage to sleep.

The other one was Rydekar.

The last three days had been an unending stream of politics from dusk to dawn. The lords and ladies of every court had come to bestow gifts and renew their vows of fealty to the high crown of their respective kingdoms. Rissa spent most of it with Rydekar, but they were never alone.

She hadn't so much as discussed what she'd discovered during her trip.

"Good. You served me well, Morgan. I'll see that Rye doesn't neglect to reward you." The woman must have flown for days nonstop to locate her friends for her.

"Actually, there's one thing I wish to ask of you." The spy hesitated.

"Well?" Rissa smiled reassuringly, though her answer was noncommittal.

"I'd like to be considered for your household,

my lady." Awkwardly, Morgan glanced at Rydekar. "I'm content as the spymaster of Tenebris, but my heart has long told me I may not quite belong to the unseelie world. I don't enjoy...havoc."

Rissa laughed, because she liked a bit of havoc herself. "Rydekar and I will discuss the matter and get back to you."

Morgan bowed and retreated into the distance.

"How diplomatic," Rye said, playful. "One might think you were born for politics, my queen."

She stuck her tongue out. How he liked to remind her she'd been a stubborn idiot for no reason. She was suited to her role. Now she didn't expect someone to scream at her to give the crown back, she found that she enjoyed it, too.

"Your queen?" Rissa echoed.

Rydekar rolled his eyes, leading the way.

To her surprise, he was heading to the tower, rather than the throne hall.

"Aren't we holding court?"

Rydekar hesitated. "We could, but it would be respectful to spend the rest of the night in mourning."

She didn't need to be told twice. Rissa rushed up the stairs eagerly. She'd barely had a moment to herself for days.

"In a hurry?" Rye seemed amused.

"I have a bathing pool waiting for me."

"Care for some company?"

She glanced over her shoulder. "I don't see why not."

Back in her room, she entered her pool without bothering to remove her silk dress. Rissa sighed in delight when warmth engulfed her.

After swimming from one end to the other, she rested her back against the edge of the pool.

"I thought you were joining me?" she asked.

Rydekar had remained at the door, leaning against the frame.

"I'm trying."

She frowned up at him, confused and perhaps a little hurt. He had to force himself to walk into her room?

"Well, get in or go out. I don't like keeping doors open."

After a moment of hesitation, he stepped inside, and kicked the door closed behind him, but he wasn't approaching her either.

"Are you going to stare at me forever, or spill what's on your mind?"

"Both, in all likelihood." He stuffed his hand in his pocket. "I failed you."

Rissa blinked. "Sorry?"

"At the end, I failed you." He shook his head in self-disgust. "Though I failed you long before. I shouldn't have let you go north. I should have insisted you remain here and—"

"And I would have done what I pleased either way," Rissa interrupted. "I'm not your subject, Rye."

"No, but you're *mine* to protect." The way he insisted on the word "mine" was telling. He knew. He knew he was her mate.

She closed her eyes. "If you'd kept me here, you would have had to keep me captive. I would have resented it, and you. I wouldn't have understood a thing. Titus raised me as well as he knew how, but I was isolated and naïve. I knew little of Denarhelm. I still need to know so much more. I needed to travel, see, and understand things myself." There was more. "I needed to learn to believe in myself. And I couldn't have done that if you'd cut my wings. You were exactly what I needed: an ideal to strive toward." He was in control, calm, organized, and responsible—everything that a seelie queen ought to be.

"Some ideal. I passed out. *Tharsen* banished the sea queen, not I."

So that was his true problem. Rissa rolled her eyes. "I passed out too. Tharsen helped me *too*. And he wouldn't have been here to do so had you not come to find me in my woods, and supported my choice to go wake him up." He might have been grumpy about it, but he'd still supported her.

"Listen to me, Rydekar Bane. You haven't failed me. Not once."

He nodded.

"Say it. I want to hear the words."

"Bossy," he chided.

Rissa glared.

With a sigh, Rye repeated after her, "I haven't failed you."

She grinned. "Good. Now come. The water's perfect."

He kicked his boots off and removed his coat, doublet, and shirt, revealing his sculptural, tanned skin. Next, he lowered his velvet breeches. Unlike the first time she'd watched him undress, he wore nothing underneath. Modesty might dictate that she avert her eyes, but Rissa found that she wasn't inclined to.

Rydekar was perfection, inch after inch.

She stared as he stalked to the pool, and lowered himself in.

"By the gods, this is some pool." He threw his head back and moaned, before looking back to her.

Wet, his hair looked almost brown .

"You shouldn't have shown me. You'll have to share now."

"I think I'll survive you." Rissa watched him disappear under the surface of the water and trailed his shadow. He reappeared inches away from her.

"I'm not sure I'll survive you," he replied, edging forward with a deliberate languor.

She shuddered, breathing out hard.

He kissed her softly, tentatively. Her heart raced, gripped by something not unlike panic, only darker, more urgent. His hands slid up her arms and settled on either side of her, caging her in. "In fact, I know I won't."

Rissa blinked. "What?"

She'd never know; the next moment, Rydekar deepened his kiss, his hard chest pressing against her, and she forgot everything, right down to who and what she was. All she knew was that she wanted more.

Desperation. That was what drove her heart into a frenzy; she was desperate for more, terrified that this embrace would ever end.

She wrapped her legs around him and one of his hands moved to support her back. Pressing to him, to the hardness of his shaft, she stifled a moan, grinding against it as their mouths danced together, tongues teasing and clashing. Desire unfurled inside her, wilder than sunfire, stronger than pain, fear, or anything she'd ever felt.

Rye groaned, tearing his head back with reticence. "You need to know—"

"I need to feel." She pressed her mouth to his, hungrily claiming it back.

His hands trembling, Rydekar fumbled with the ties at the front of her dress, attempting to make sense of its knots. She barked a laugh, because she never would have imagined him fumbling at anything.

"Let me." She unhooked the top, spilling her breasts free.

Rydekar grunted, bending to take one nipple in his hot mouth. Rissa breathed between clenched teeth, waves of pleasure hitting one after the next.

"By the gods..." She threw her head back to the floor. He was so gifted with his tongue.

Rye slid the rest of her out of the pool, until her hips rested against the hard stone. He spread her legs apart and buried his face between them. Then he sucked, and licked, and teased her with his fingers as she writhed. Rissa screamed herself hoarse, each ministration driving her closer to madness.

"Please!" she begged, like she'd never begged, her body quivering with need. Her fingers threaded through his dark locks of hair, so when he straightened up, she lifted her torso with his, sitting up against him.

Rye slid both hands along her legs and lifted them with her long skirt. "I'm going to take you now, Serissa. When I do, know I am claiming you, body and soul, for the rest of our days."

Gods, yes, please yes.

She didn't realize she'd said the words out loud until he laughed. The head of his cock pressed against the apex of her thighs, and though her entire body seemed made of liquid fire, he still felt like steel when his long shaft entered her in one swift, hard thrust. He captured her yelp in a soft kiss, reverent and caring, all the while drawing back to ram back home, hard and fast again.

"Mine. You're mine." He repeated the word with each punishing thrust and she panted, white-hot pleasure building higher and higher in a maddening crescendo. "Say it!"

"Yours!"

Rye grunted in approval, thrusting increasingly faster and deeper. She couldn't see, couldn't hear, couldn't do anything but *feel* more and more, and more, till they both reached a sharp precipice and fell.

Her long scream drowned his deep groan, then she was limp against him, utterly spent.

She couldn't even describe what they'd just done. Sex didn't begin to cover it. She'd had sex before; it was nothing like this.

His chest rose and fell fast along with hers.

"I claim you right back," she whispered.

Her mate. Her partner.

Her king.

Rydekar gathered her in his arms and carried her to her bed, drenched and soiled. He peeled her dress off her, before kissing every inch of her body, and making love to her again, and again, and again.

EPILOGUE

"We're never having sex again."

Rydekar chuckled. It wasn't the first time Rissa had said so. In fact, it was the seventh time in the years since they'd found each other. She might even have believed it at the time.

He kissed the top of her head.

"I mean it this time, we're done. I'm not having another child."

He ignored her, bouncing their newborn daughter in his arms.

Rissa glared at him. "Didn't anyone tell you fae aren't supposed to reproduce this much?"

"Mommy's tired, Dawn, darling. Ignore her. We know you want a little brother to play with."

"In your dreams!" she snarled.

He laughed, carrying the baby to her bed before returning to his mate's side.

They'd ruled together in the Old Keep for five centuries so far, their high court overseeing both Tenebris and Denarhelm. There had been times of war, times of peace, betrayal, near-misses with death, but also joy and merriments. With this seventh child, their line was secured several times over. The one chink in their world was the shadow of the sea.

His father, Havryll, Nyla.

The girl was still alive—their spies had confirmed it—and so long as that queen ruled her courts, their world wasn't safe. Rydekar doubted that she'd attack them head-on, not until she was certain she could win. She was unreachable to them in the depths of the ocean, but until the threat she represented was dealt with, he had to remain vigilant.

Rydekar knew their eldest daughter was eager to take the unseelie crown, but how could he hand it to her, knowing she'd inherit a war that had started before she drew breath?

Rissa was hoping their third son might take the seelie crown, though like her, he was reluctant to assume the responsibility.

A new child meant that they'd stay another few decades in this world, but both of them were getting restless, eager to go wandering the other greater universe, like their ancestors had done before them.

"She's asleep."

"You're a child whisperer," Rissa pouted, quite jealous of his ability to calm their children.

He ought to confess he used his mental ability to compel them into sleep, someday. Perhaps not for the next few years, lest she demand he stop doing it.

"Perhaps I can become a nanny, if the kingly business gets tedious."

She chuckled as he lay down next to her.

"We did well with this one. She's pretty, like her mother."

"And strong, like her father," Rissa retorted.

Rydekar yawned. Rissa had gone into labor late in the night, and now it was almost dusk. She caressed his forehead, just as exhausted as him. "Sleep, my mate."

"Right after you, my nightmare."

The End

ACKNOWLEDGMENTS

Being an author is a solitary journey if you let yourself hide in your writing cave. I've made that mistake in the past. Now, I've opened up to my readers through May Sage's Coven, and interacting with you guys is incredibly motivating. Thank you for reminding me my work is loved, when I'm getting unmotivated!

The Cursed Crown started its journey several years ago. I actually pitched it to my agent, before deciding that I wanted to stay in control of Rissa and Rydekar's journey. From the very start, my editor Theresa has been cheering me on. She's the mirror I bounce most of my ideas off. She's even more present in this story, because Rydekar's character is basically based on her—a highly efficient, organized mind who can be morally gray for the greater good. They're the epitome of seelie folk.

I also thank Sylvia Frost for her support. She's been reading bits and pieces of this book for ages, and demanding more.

And finally, thank *you* for supporting me <3

NEXT IN FANTASY ROMANCE
FROM MAY SAGE AS ALEXI
BLAKE:

So Sweet the Bite.

A ruthless prince.

The second-born heir of Aevar, Alessandre is the sword of the realm, bound to protect the crown from all enemies. With spies sneaking from the southern and eastern kingdoms, demons swarming from the darklands, and traitors scheming at every corner, he's grown hard as stone and unbending as steel.

Until she came, muddling his black-and-white world.

A jaded witch.

The last black witch in a time when dark magic is forbidden under penalty of death, Valina has learned to embrace shades of gray to survive.

She's retreated to the darklands for a

hundred years, but a shadow from her past disrupts her refuge. She has to once again intertwine with the royal court and all its machinations. Poison, lies, and secrets threaten the rule of the new queen.

An unlikely alliance.

Valina's very existence goes against the laws Alessandre enforces. She was hunted by men like him for decades. They can't help being at each other's throats, despite their explosive attraction.

When an old enemy rises, ready to strike, Alessandre and Valina have to attempt to call a temporary truce in order to defend their worlds.

So Sweet the Bite *is a sensual fantasy standalone novel, unsuitable for sensitive readers.*